The Hunter's Curse

Ashley Felts

Copyright © 2023

ISBN: 978-1-959670-83-4

Dedication

To my loving and supportive husband,
Patrick

Acknowledgment

Write My Wrongs

Contents

About the Author

Ashley is a a major in meteorology and an animal lover.". She quickly decided after college that writing was her passion. With a million ideas to get on paper, it's only a matter of time before one of them is a hit.

Chapter 1

Astrid had come to this town to die. The cycle of her curse was coming to a close, so she'd decided to lay low for a while and call a small town her home for the next few months. She'd never lived there before, but Marcello, her only friend, insisted it would be a nice place to call home.

It had a sweet downtown that could be easily walked through. Most people had a car, but walking was the most common method of transportation. Locals would greet each other as they passed.

Residents often gathered for lunch at one of the two quaint diners located on the outskirts of downtown. In the evening, the diners transformed into crowded bars, where people would drink and eat their day away. One other bar flourished in the middle of downtown: The Casket. Although it had a terribly uninviting name, it was a nicer bar that served mixed drinks and better quality food. That was the place for special occasions: birthdays, weddings, and the like.

Astrid made it a habit of inserting herself into a new small town every few years or so. Even though the States wasn't her favorite place to live in the world, they were an interesting one. She liked the sites and the language and enjoyed watching how everything changed so dramatically all the time. It didn't remind her of home, but it made her happy enough.

She had traveled a lot during her lives, exploring Europe mostly, but about one hundred years prior, she'd ventured her way across the Pacific into North America, and she wasn't planning on leaving anytime soon. She was a social butterfly, always chatting with people, taking in the local life, and enjoying every moment she had to explore.

Although she didn't keep to herself, she wasn't in the habit of making friends either; too many bad experiences.

Astrid was a little over the average height for a girl, with crisp, long, dirty-blond hair that she often put into a small disheveled bun on her head. She didn't like the length of her hair, but it was impossible to change it. She was too far along in this cycle of her curse.

Her eyes were green and dark, her hands delicate and soft. She dazzled with beauty but had a way of hiding her radiance, almost as if she could turn it on and off; one moment she was stunning, and the next, she was an average beauty someone might not even give a second glance to, even though she looked exactly the same.

Her friend, Marcello, on the other hand, was not one for looks. He had plain shoulder-length brown hair with an average face that rarely changed its simple expression. At first glance, people could never tell if he was angry, tired, or bored. He was tall and thin but toned; every muscle was on display if he wore the right clothes… or no clothes. He often donned well-made dark-brown suits with some sort of off-color collarless shirt underneath.

Despite his unfriendly appearance and lackluster personality, he was an angel to Astrid. He'd always been by her side throughout the many years her curse had been in place. He was the only one who never forgot her, making him the only one who still cared. Through every cycle of her curse, he would wait for her; he protected her, loved her, and cared for her. They were soulmates without benefits since they were strictly friends.

He'd chosen the town because of its friendly, historically-driven qualities as well as its location close to a nearby college. The small place was called Blessings, Colorado. Astrid found the name hysterically amusing. But she was excited to move there. She was ready to relax; hunting could be a very tiring lifestyle, even when one's strengths surpassed some of the oldest vampires.

Astrid was a vampire hunter, or, at least, when she turned sixteen, she always became one. It was an instant upgrade from a normal person to an extraordinary person. Marcello, however, was a vampire. It made their relationship even more interesting when they explained it to people: a vampire hunter who was best friends with a vampire.

Even though Astrid identified with the title, she didn't just go around ripping out every vampire's heart. She looked for the bad ones: the ones who killed only for fun, tortured people, or abused their vampire powers and strengths.

Astrid couldn't really judge the ones who were just trying to live their immortal lives in peace; she had done some bad things she was not proud of, and they haunted her every day, along with her curse. But she tried to keep the extremist vampires in check. She'd gone through phases throughout her lives of not caring, but she was trying to use her strengths productively.

However, Marcello and Astrid had grown up together before they both began their seemingly never-ending lives. They were best friends since birth. Even when both of their futures took a turn for the worse, they pulled each other out of the darkness. As for Astrid's curse… well, she didn't like to talk about it. She'd been trying to break it for over two thousand years with no success.

However, on that day, she wasn't thinking about her curse. Instead, she was thinking about her first day of the spring semester at Bella Sleigh College, just five miles north of Blessings. It was a petite college resting right below a tall mountain. From a distance, it looked like a small kingdom growing out of the trees. It reminded her of her favorite city in Italy, Assisi, which rested sweetly on the side of Monte Subasio and was made almost entirely of white-and-tan stone bricks. Bella Sleigh had a similar look and feel but was more modern. It was only a few decades old, whereas Assisi was two thousand or so. Nonetheless, the college was beautiful.

Astrid was expecting a rather normal first day of school: meeting new people, listening to boring professor speeches about what the class would teach her, and getting lost traversing from class to class. Although Astrid had done her fair share of traveling, she was not keen on map reading or directions. She often let Marcello lead when they traveled, or she just roamed until she came upon a new city, town, or ocean. There was no need to read maps when she was wandering.

That day, though, she would probably get lost. When the sun was up, Marcello had to stay inside, or he'd die. Vampires didn't do well in the sun. The worst part was it wasn't an instant death; every vampire had a critical sun exposure point. If a vampire was in the sun for too long—an amount of time that varied for every vampire depending on age—then they would continue to burn even after fleeing to the shadows. The older they were, the quicker they'd burn. In Marcello's case, it wouldn't take long in the sun for it to be too late.

But it was a pretty normal day starting off—not to confuse Astrid's life for normal, though. Since Astrid didn't sleep very much, she woke up with the late Spring sun. She then went to harass Marcello as he tried to get to sleep. It was almost impossible to disturb a vampire when the sun was up, but Astrid knew a few tricks to bother Marcello.

As she entered his room, she saw Marcello resting on his oversized bed. He lay still on his back, with one arm stretched out and reaching above his head while the other rested gently on his stomach. He looked more peaceful than normal, so Astrid decided to be kind and let him sleep. The only way for Marcello to have the ability to sleep in the house and not a coffin, grave, or hole in the ground was for them to board up all the windows on the second floor of the house to allow no light to pass through, particularity in Marcello's room. They also kept all the shutters on the outside of the house closed to hide the boards and make the house look normal.

They lived on the outskirts of a large pond about two miles from downtown in a house that most would describe as a cottage. It was white and wooden, stained with dirt and yellow pollen; a wraparound porch encompassed most of the house. The second floor even had its own balcony attached to Astrid's room. There was no garage, just a long gravel driveway that connected to the main road on the back side.

It was an old place Marcello had lived in a few decades before while he waited for Astrid's memory to return during one of her curse's cycles.

She had only lived there for a month, but the inside was already clean and all boxes were unpacked. Every inch of the house was ready to be lived in; Astrid had made sure of that. Although there wasn't much to be unpacked anyway—they traveled light—she hated a dirty or cluttered house. Wherever her home might be, it was always her place of peace. It was the place she came to relax, wind down, and de-stress. Clutter and messes did not allow for that.

The inside was worn like the outside, but clean. The furniture and appliances were outdated, but still in working order and useful. The couches looked like they came out of the Victorian era and vibrant tapestries hung from the walls. The downstairs consisted of a small guest room and bathroom, a decent-sized kitchen, and a large living area, while the upstairs had one large room with a bathroom for Astrid and a smaller sun-proof room for Marcello.

As she left Marcello alone to sleep, she went downstairs to the kitchen to make the usual breakfast for herself: eggs, grapefruit, toast, and black coffee. She used to be such a picky eater, but she'd started eating mostly the same thing every day. One thing she was particular about was her coffee. It had to be fresh and recently roasted. She made sure to buy whole beans, and she always ground them herself at home.

She made her coffee, sipped it while she slowly ate on her porch downstairs, and wondered how her day would go.

After she finished her breakfast, packed her things for class, and made her way to the door, she was suddenly alert. Something felt odd in the air; maybe it was a smell or a sound she noticed from her heightened senses. Whatever it was, it put her on edge and made her anxious. But she wasn't going to stay inside because of an uneasy feeling, especially if it could be nothing. Maybe she had forgotten something and her subconscious suddenly remembered, giving her a twang of discomfort as her conscious struggled to think of what it could be. So she threw on her backpack, slipped on her tan leather-bound sandals, and went cautiously out the door.

***

It was a pleasant walk to the campus, although it was more of a run. Part of the perks of being a magically-induced vampire hunter was the speed. She could get almost anywhere in the blink of an eye.

Astrid essentially had to be faster, stronger, smarter, and a better fighter than even the most well-aged vampires. Not only were humans suddenly transformed into super-humans when they became vampires, but as they aged, their strengths increased. Astrid was skilled at hunting the older vampires—so much so that most of the time, the younger vampires were the ones to catch her off guard. She saw them as no threat and as weak, so she paid less attention to them. She had learned over the years to consider every vampire as equal threats. But still, every once in a while, she would let her guard down.

As she reached the small campus, she slowed to a normal pace behind a pink cherry blossom tree. It was mid-May, so the trees were still in bloom. There was something very calming to her about them. When she had a lot of time on her hands, those were always the ones she chose to sit under, wasting her day with dreamy thoughts.

She had visited Japan once during the blooming season of the cherry blossoms. She stopped by a tranquil garden located in a green river valley where a monastery was built. The river intertwined for a few acres behind the monastery, and along all the banks were sweet cherry blossom trees; she spent three days wandering the river banks, getting lost in the beautiful blossoms.

Leaving her reverie, she walked normally over to the first stone building she saw on the campus.

Crap, she thought. She'd forgotten to print off a map; she was already as good as lost.

She read the sign on the building: Browns Building. That was good news. According to her schedule, which she had printed, she had a class there. But it wasn't until the afternoon. Right then, she was looking for Reynolds Hall.

After a quick glance, Astrid noticed a small information sign standing directly to her left. She examined it quickly and made her way to what was hopefully her destination. Her first class was Spanish, and the sign on the front of the building confirmed she was in the correct place. The building stood out from the rest because it was a dark-red brick building, not tan or off-white stone like the rest, and it was shaped like a church; there was even a bell tower at the top. Astrid scampered up the few brick steps, entering quickly through the tall wooden doors.

Whether by choice or not, that day, she'd turned on her stunning beauty. Her eyes, accompanied by her sweet innocent smile, met a few helpless souls. It wasn't a second-glance kind of day, more like a stop-in-the-middle-of-the-hall-and-stare kind of day. She couldn't say she didn't like it. Some days she liked the attention, while on others she wanted to be left alone. But it was an optimistic day, so she didn't mind the glances.

However, as she stepped swiftly through the halls, she herself was stopped in her tracks like the people who were lucky enough to catch her sweet glance; there was a smell. Not a bad smell, but a distinct one. A smell she knew very well: vampire blood.

She could literally smell it a mile away. That must have been what caught her attention that morning. Although the blood of every vampire and person had its own unique smell, there was a very noticeable difference between a vampire and a human; humans smelled of sugar and metals, while vampires smelled like fiery magic. There wasn't another way for Astrid to describe the smell of vampire blood. It smelled and tasted different for every person. It was almost like smelling air after a Summer rain, nice and sweet.

The scent worried Astrid because it meant a vampire was close. But what worried her even more was that vampires only really carried their scent when they were awake and moving around, which meant there was an alert vampire somewhere in the building. She didn't know how one could be active with the lights coming in from all the doors and windows.

Her first guess was the janitor's closet, or maybe a basement if the building had one; the vampire had to be somewhere where no sunlight could reach. She had a decision to make: miss her first day of Spanish to look for a hiding vampire, or ignore the smell and deal with it later.

And then she saw him, walking down the hall, unaffected by the sun bursting through every window and open door. She stood there standing, staring, mouth wide open. He caught her glance, made eye contact, and walked straight up to her with an alluring smirk on his face.

"Can I help you with something?"

Chapter 2

Astrid stood there speechless, completely caught off guard. There was a vampire staring her in the face during broad daylight, looking at her with those seductive eyes; he smelled sweet, like a crisp morning breeze right at dawn.

After a few awkward moments of staring and some quick thinking, she finally spoke.

"No, I'm fine," she replied as she tried to play off her awkward blunder. "I just had some really intense déjà vu."

"Funny, I think I did too," he slyly whispered.

"I'm headed to Beginner's Spanish," Astrid said, trying to make conversation. She was intrigued by the day-walking vampire—a little concerned, but more curious and excited. She'd seen so many things throughout the years that she always welcomed something new.

He gave her an obviously fake surprised look and said, "How convenient, so am I."

Astrid could tell he was lying. He was trying to be alluring and persuasive, but Astrid was immune to those types of tricks that vampires possessed. She didn't mind him trying to flirt with her, though. If he liked her, it would be easier to find out what kind of vampire he was; the kind she had to kill, or the kind who she could leave to live their long lives.

"I'm Astrid."

"Beautiful name. I'm Carter. It's a pleasure," he said as he reached out to shake her hand. She had found her vampire, and he wasn't what Astrid had excepted. She reached out and began holding his ice-cold hand. He reminded her of an anime character. He had a defined jaw and bright blue eyes. His hair was long and black, but he kept it tied back. He was taller than her but only by a few inches. He wore black dress pants, a white button-up shirt, and black suspenders—she'd never seen anyone look so good in suspenders.

Although he was overdressed for a simple college class, he wore it well.

Sensing that their handshake had gone on too long, Astrid pulled away. They stood there in silence for a moment then Astrid awkwardly asked, "So… do you know where to go to get to class?"

***

After being led to class by a vampire, her first day of Spanish had a whole new feel. Astrid could barely focus with such an unusual specimen sitting right beside her.

A new layer of interest was added on when the professor called role to make sure everyone had made it to their first day of class; Carter's name wasn't on the list.

"The office administrator told me to just go ahead and go to class and she would register me later."

His words caused even the professor to swoon a little. Vampires rarely had to use their forceful persuasion trick to get people to do things; most of the time, their natural charm was enough. In that case, there was no persuasion necessary, just the sound of his elegant voice.

"O-okay… just talk to me after class," the professor stumbled. She was petite, had curly blonde hair, was wearing all pink, and didn't have a chance against his charm.

Persuasion was one of the many perks of being a vampire. Although they had to drink blood—or most had to, anyway— and they couldn't come out during the day, Astrid considered most of the things vampires could do as perks compared to the normal qualities humans had. The basics were super speed and strength, unmatchable reflexes, highly enhanced senses, quick healing, and persuasion. Persuasion was a perk because simply by looking into a human's eyes, a vampire could make them do anything. Technically, immortality could be considered a perk, but that was a tricky one. Some considered it a perk, while others thought it was a curse. Part of Astrid's curse was a form of immortality, so her opinion on that was already set: she hated it. But Astrid didn't really consider vampire's immortal because they could be killed. There was nothing, really, that she thought was truly immortal, except maybe gods and Naturals (which was the proper name for a witch or wizard), but she'd never met a god. Even after a Natural died, their soul continued to be able to communicate with the living forever, as if they never really passed. But right then, Astrid was more concerned with why that vampire could walk in the day.

She didn't have a complete plan yet on how to extract his day-walking secret from him, but she knew it started off with befriending Carter. However, for some reason, she was finding it harder to resist his alluring glow. Sitting next to him made her shiver.

He was such an exciting creature, a vampire walking in the sun. Discovering his secrets was going to be much more fun than sitting around waiting to die from her curse.

Luckily for Astrid, the professor assigned a long-term group project on the first day of class. No one else really cared who their partners were except Astrid and Carter; they simultaneously looked at each other when she asked if anyone had a partner they would prefer.

However, Astrid wasn't sure why he was so interested in her. She knew his secret of being a vampire and his uniqueness of being a day-walker, but all he knew about her was her name. Then, she suddenly realized why he was so curious: when he first asked if he could help her with anything, she paused. At that moment, he had been trying to persuade her, and it didn't work. If it had, she would have answered immediately.

His interest in her would make things a little bit more complicated. He was probably going to try and be sneaky to see if he could get any dirt on her, risking her being exposed as a hunter. However, she still considered herself to have the better end of the deal. For all he knew, she was just a human with some glitch making her unable to be persuaded.

But Astrid's eventful day didn't end with Carter.

When Spanish class was over, the two exchanged numbers and agreed to meet at his house the next evening to get started on their project. She packed up her things and began to make her way to her next class: Intro Psychology. She was only taking three classes that semester: those two and Intro Sociology. She chose Spanish because, despite all of the languages she knew, Spanish was not one of them. She decided it was time to learn.

However, although she had taken some sociology and psychology classes a few years ago, she always liked to keep up to date on how people thought. It was how she stayed alive as a hunter. Knowing what people were going to do and how they would react could be the difference between life and death. Of course, her deaths were only temporary.

Her psychology class was in the Browns Building, which she had found earlier in the day. If she could just remember how to get there, she would be fine. She had some time to kill between the two classes, so she wandered around until she found the cherry tree she had discovered earlier. She sat down to let her scrambled thoughts try and answer the mystery of the day-walking vampire. And then she saw them.

Standing only two hundred feet away, sharing secrets on the quad, was Carter and two other vampires. She was shocked again. For some reason, she had never considered that there may be more than one day-walker. She assumed it was a unique fluke that separated him from other vampires. But there they were, all three of them, chatting on the quad in broad daylight.

***

That evening, Astrid waited anxiously for Marcello to wake. She sat impatiently on the top balcony until the sun completely disappeared over the horizon, watching as the darkness quickly moved in.

Marcello awoke right on schedule, and after searching the house, he eventually made his way to the seat next to Astrid on the balcony. Before he had a second to speak, she speed-talked her way through the story of her day, making sure to describe in vivid detail that the vampires were walking in the sun. She was giddy with curiosity and excitement. Marcello, however, was not as amused.

He was a better judge of character than Astrid was, and he generally didn't like vampires. Although he was one himself, he considered himself evolved. Most vampires chose to ignore their gifts, whereas Marcello used them to better the world. Unfortunately, "bettering the world" meant killing his own kind since they were the most menacing and outgoing of the supernatural creatures.

Most other beings kept to themselves. They didn't like humans knowing about them, and they often kept out of the lives of humans. But vampires were meddlers; they liked to stand out, get in trouble, and make a scene. That was why the day-walkers were particularly threatening to Marcello; not only could these vampires walk in the sun, but they lived very connected to the human world. That generally meant danger for the humans—like becoming afternoon snacks.

Marcello thought of two reasons the vampires could be walking in the sun. The first was that they may be Energies.

Energies were a type of vampire who drained what best could be described as souls. They stole victims' life energy. He and Astrid didn't like talking about Energies. They weren't her specialty, and they were very dangerous. However, there were only a few of them. Unlike blood vampires, Energies couldn't create protégées. There were very few, and they could never generate any more offspring (as far as she knew), which was a good thing. They also rarely came out in public, although they could walk in the sun.

Astrid had experience with most of the Energies; they were so rare that she knew almost all of them. However, she was pretty sure Carter and his crew weren't Energies simply from their smell. That left one other plausible explanation: Naturals. It didn't make much sense because Naturals hated vampires. Astrid had even seen the soul of a dead Natural build an army to try and wipe out vampires. They were unfortunately unsuccessful, but it was a good example of how much they detested each other. Even her own curse was caused because of the feud between Naturals and vampires. Her many lives were the result of an angry Natural. So it would be strange if a Natural was helping a vampire.

However, it was the twenty-first century, and Naturals weren't as close-knit as they used to be. Maybe one had been left out of the vampire-hating loop and befriended the three

Astrid had seen on the quad. She hoped it was just three. But what Marcello said next really surprised her.

"I think you should leave it alone," he said decisively. "The easiest way to find out would be to befriend them. But you're too far along in this curse cycle to make friends. It would just complicate things."

Astrid had forgotten to mention she had already partnered up with Carter for her Spanish project and was going to his house the next night.

Just as she finished explaining that detail to Marcello and his face flashed with irritation, Astrid's phone rang before he could get out another word. She examined the number and grinned from ear to ear.

"No!" Marcello asserted. "Don't answer it." But he was too late.

"Hello?" Astrid said curiously.

"Astrid? This is Carter," he proclaimed.

She smiled more, while Marcello continued to look more and more displeased.

"I was curious if you wanted to go out this evening, maybe to The Casket? Tonight we could play and tomorrow we could work," he teased.

It certainly piqued her interest, although Marcello was shaking his head vehemently; he clearly didn't approve. She gave him a smile and a wink then agreed to Carter's flirtatious plan. It was a little past 9:00 p.m. She thought it was strange he would suggest hanging out so late on a weeknight. But then again, he was a vampire.

She got ready quickly and half-heartedly listened to Marcello try to convince her to stay home and drop her new investigation. She didn't like ignoring Marcello or making him mad, but it was one of those nights when she just didn't care. It also irritated her that he would bring her curse into things. Making a friend wouldn't make anything more complicated. It just meant she'd spend less time with him.

And then she felt bad. Once the cycle of her curse was over in three months, Marcello wouldn't see her for another sixteen years, and she wouldn't remember him even if he saw her before. But it was too late now. She was too curious and was not about to change her plans. So she apologized to Marcello, gave him a quick kiss on the cheek, and bolted to the middle of downtown where Carter was waiting.

Chapter 3

Since Carter didn't know anything about her, she had to walk more slowly than she wanted; she needed to move at a human speed. What a drag, she thought. Although Astrid enjoyed leisurely activities, she hated moving slowly. She didn't like wasting time when she had to be somewhere or something exciting was going to happen.

Halfway there, Astrid began regretting her decision to walk; a car would have been much faster since she had to maintain such a slow pace. Suddenly, she heard a faint chime from her purse: a text from Carter asking if she was still coming. "Figures," she said out loud. He probably ran there.

When she finally arrived, it was a little past 9:30. She walked into the well-kept bar and scanned the crowd for Carter. She was taken aback when she saw his eyes staring right into hers from across the room. She sauntered over to his table with an innocent smile on her face.

Most of the time, Astrid followed Marcello's lead in areas with overactive vampire activity. They would travel to those places together and access the best way to handle the distasteful vampires. It often ended in multiple deaths.

However, she couldn't really judge them just because they were vampires. They weren't all bad. And besides, the whole reason she was cursed involved her doing much more terrible acts than most vampires could dream of.

It was strange because, although vampires were not officially discovered, a lot of people knew they existed. They just didn't talk about it.

Sometimes, a vampire would threaten a human's life and their family's lives if they ever told anyone. Sometimes, it was just such a good secret, like a vampire best friend or lover that only they knew about. People often wished something amazing would happen to them, especially if nothing ever did. For those people who had met vampires, it was like being a part of a secret club. It made them feel unique, so they kept the secret.

Unfortunately, things were getting a little more complicated than that. The news was starting to take notice of a well-hidden supernatural world that existed all around them; people were starting to look for those types of stories.

However, it wasn't something Astrid had any time to worry about. Since she only had a few months left before her current life ended, she would just have to wait and see what happened when she regained her memory in the new cycle. With the way technology was advancing, she wondered what it would be like in sixteen years.

"Good thing I don't have class tomorrow." He greeted her condescendingly for being late but with a teasing smile on his face.

The comment took her by surprise; Astrid didn't like being talked down to, even if he was just teasing. It caused her to react too quickly and without thinking.

"How did you get here so fast?" she asked, unhesitant. "Do you have some superhuman speed I don't know about?" Astrid realized she'd said too much, but she kept her calm demeanor.

Although slightly taken aback, Carter rebutted with the answer Astrid had completely forgotten existed. "I drove," he said, pointing out the window to his parked car across the street. Astrid let out a faint awkward laugh.

She sat down at the four-person table, making sure to sit across from him instead of next to him. She didn't want him to get any ideas… yet.

Astrid ordered a cheap glass of red wine and Carter ordered a top shelf whiskey, which she knew was just for show. Although vampires could technically eat human food, most of them were too disgusted by the taste to even swallow it. Only the older vampires were able to put on a good performance.

Which brought Astrid to her next question: how old was he? She'd never get a true answer if she asked, but she could often tell a vampire's age after spending enough time with them.

She decided to talk about basic interests for a bit. Astrid began and admitted she liked to watch movies, drink wine, clean, read books, and drink coffee; she liked to relax. She didn't tell Carter, but her body was almost always on overdrive and ready to fight, so she tried to do relaxing things as often as she could to calm her nerves.

However, Carter said he liked the more active things: running, hiking, swimming, and so on. He basically liked to always be moving. That was one of the clues she was looking for; Carter was a young vampire.

She used "young" loosely. It could mean he was as young as a newborn or as old as three hundred. He was probably still overwhelmed by his new strengths and required a lot of external activity to release his built-up energy. That didn't mean that older vampires didn't have a lot of energy, but their bodies had adapted; they were often calmer but much more dangerous.

Astrid was more like the older vampires. She had plenty of energy, but she kept it under control mentally, not by physically releasing it.

"I like doing relaxing things too," he said almost shyly. He was flirting, but Astrid kept her cool.

Their drinks took longer than expected to arrive, and Carter gave a sad, regretful look when he got his; there was definitely another liquid he wished was in that glass.

He began to look at Astrid suspiciously once she got her drink; he was analyzing her. He was trying to decide if she was a vampire or not. So, she looked him straight in the eyes, with a defiant smile on her face, and gave him an enjoying look as she tasted her glass of wine.

Most of the time, vampires could tell when someone else was a vampire, but every once in a while, a vampire didn't have the normal giveaways and blended in with humans. Carter obviously suspected Astrid of being one of those hidden vampires.

"Cabernets are my favorite," she said, looking at the glass, emphasizing the word "favorite."

"They do look the most appealing," Carter whispered, examining the dark red color as she swirled it in her glass.

She almost laughed but kept her composure.

"How old are you?" Astrid asked, curious how he would answer.

He answered methodically, as if he'd said it a hundred times, practicing for sincerity and perfection. "I'm twenty-five. And you?"

"Twenty-four," she answered honestly. Although her answer was more complicated than that, by saying she was twenty-four, she definitely wasn't lying.

As she took another sip of her wine and Carter doubtfully examined his whiskey, a curious figure walked through the door, followed by three more.

The first person to walk through the door Astrid knew all too well. It was Marcello, probably coming to check up on her, although she was more than capable of defending herself.

Of the next three who walked in, she recognized two; they were the other vampires from the school. They gave Carter a suspicious and eager look as they walked in, almost nodding to him to join them. He looked a bit concerned but not enough that he was going to leave their table.

One of the vampires was a man and the other was a woman. The woman looked at her and Astrid immediately saw a few drops of blood around her month. The woman must have noticed because she quickly wiped her mouth with her hand and looked away from Astrid. She had long bright-red hair that she kept in a tight braid resting down her back. Her skin was darker than most and made her bright hair stand out even more. Her eyes were a piercing green, and she was rather tall. For a vampire, she wore pretty conservative clothing. She was probably young and hadn't yet come into her seductive vampire persona.

Her hair and eyes had probably morphed when she had been turned; most vampires experienced a few physical changes during their transformation.

The man was about the female's height and had bright-blond hair, but it was cut short and slightly spiked up in the middle. His eyes were a deadly dark-brown color that caused Astrid to feel uneasy when looking directly into them.

Astrid found the woman to be much more attractive than the man. She seemed like a young, innocent vampire, one who Astrid would hopefully never have to kill. But the man seemed dark and wild. He looked like a greedy tiger, ready to pounce at any moment. It wasn't about the food for him; it was about the kill.

The third person in the group was new to Astrid, but she knew he was… different. From his smell, stature, and shifting gaze, she guessed he was a Natural. She did notice he had beautiful dark skin.

Astrid knew a lot about Naturals. For one thing, she had severely pissed one off many years ago, so she was an expert on how to get herself cursed. And for another, she just simply had grown to befriend some Naturals and asked for their help from time to time if she was hunting some particularly difficult vampires.

She noticed that the two vampires were holding hands, and the man seemed protective over the woman. And even more interesting, she noticed the Natural man also seemed very protective of the female vampire. They both kept glancing at Marcello, and stood in between him and the female vampire with puffed up chests and sour looks. Astrid couldn't really tell whether Carter had similar protective feelings toward her, although he seemed a bit irritated when he saw them walk in.

Suddenly, Carter looked suspicious and uneasy; he was staring defensively toward Marcello. That allowed Astrid to put a few of the puzzle pieces together; when the three people she didn't know walked into the bar, the "we need to talk to you" look that they gave Carter was because of Marcello. He was a new vampire to them, which could often be very threatening, especially to those who were trying to lay low.

That gave a little bit of hope to Astrid; hopefully, those day-walking vampires were, for the most part, trying to be good citizens. However, she decided to really rock the boat between her and Carter's new relationship and invite Marcello to come to sit at their table.

When Marcello walked in, he saw Astrid almost instantly. He was wearing a medium brown suit that he almost always wore, never buttoned, and a white short-sleeved shirt underneath. His brown hair, as always, was down. Astrid gave him a big smile and waved him over to the table Carter and she were sitting at. Marcello walked over casually, while Carter stared bug-eyed as he realized Astrid was friends with another vampire. The group of three who had just come in were now sitting at the bar and decided to give a deadlier stare toward Marcello.

"What are you doing here?" Astrid asked as she sweetly smiled at him and put her hand on his arm. Deep down, she wanted to squeeze his arm as a statement that she didn't want him there, but she decided against that.

"I came to check up on you," he gently said, all the while keeping a close eye on Carter. "I thought you might want me to drive you home instead of walking all the way so late at night."

This was a comical statement for Astrid since they both knew she could run home in just a few seconds, but she thought it was sweet he was coming to check up on her. It would be even funnier once she found out he didn't even drive there, so there was no car to take her home.

"This is Carter," Astrid said, motioning toward him. "Carter, this is Marcello."

They said greetings to each other cautiously while Astrid tried not to laugh at the humor of the situation; everyone was so tense while she was just playing the part of being unaware.

"Astrid tells me you two are in the same Spanish class," Marcello said normally.

"Yes, we are, but she hasn't told me anything about you," Carter jabbed.

That seemingly put Marcello on edge, so Astrid tried to smooth out the situation a little.

"Marcello is my oldest and best friend," she insisted. "We live together a couple miles from downtown. He's always looking out for me." Astrid's attempt to take some tension out of the situation didn't work.

It wasn't about territory; it was about a lack of trust. She assumed both Marcello and Carter did not trust the other around Astrid, and the other supernatural clearly didn't trust Marcello at all. So, she tried a different approach.

"Well, it's getting late," Astrid announced, stretching her arms to appear sleepy. "Thanks for getting a drink with me. I'll see you tomorrow night at your house to work on that project." Astrid reached for her wallet to pay for her wine when Carter, fast as lightning, grabbed her hand and looked her in the eyes.

"It was such a pleasure," he whispered, "I'll pay. You have a wonderful evening. I look forward to tomorrow." He glanced at Marcello, eyes shifting to more of a glare. "Nice to meet you."

"Yes, you too. Good evening," Marcello said stiffly.

As Astrid walked out of the busy bar, she glanced over at the group of three before she left. The girl seemed sweet, giving her a gentle, friendly smile; she was definitely a young vampire, not yet come into her own. The two boys, however, gave less friendly glances, which were mostly directed toward Marcello.

As they exited the bar, they both looked around, and realizing the coast was clear, they ran home in a matter of seconds.

As they reached their front porch, Marcello looked seriously at Astrid. "I got a strange feeling in there that people were watching me," Marcello said. He wasn't normally one for humour, so that made Astrid laugh a good bit.

"No," she admitted with a smile, "I don't think you were their favorite."

"Astrid, do you know why I came to get you tonight?" Marcello asked, his tone suddenly very serious.

She shook her head, giving him a concerned look.

"I heard someone screaming. Not a long, loud scream. Just a faint, short yelp, as if someone had muffled the rest of the sound. I ran to see what was wrong. And before I got there, I smelled the blood."

Astrid became worried, although no one would have believed it from her mannerisms. She became alert, cautious, and a sly smile slithered across her face; she transformed into the hunter that she was, ready to kill. Then, a faint glimmer of sadness trickled onto her face as Marcello finished his story.

"When I made it around the corner of the back of the bar," he continued, "there was lots of spilled blood and the body of a young man on the ground. The girl vampire had killed someone, and the worst part is… they saw me."

Chapter 4

Marcello was sitting at the house doing what he did most of the time: reading, thinking, or researching. He was almost always trying to find a way to break Astrid's curse. He hated the cycles and the pain she went through every time. He wanted her to be free; she had suffered enough.

Astrid had not given up on breaking her curse, but she wasn't as invested as Marcello in finding a solution. They had tried so many things, and she'd said she was tired of being let down. But Marcello kept searching, reading book after book. He had a list of authors who were categorized as fiction writers but actually knew about supernatural creatures or were one themselves. His list of authors was constantly growing, which meant he was constantly reading and hoping to find a clue as to how to break her curse.

On that particular evening, he felt like he was wasting his time. Nothing he was reading had any relevant information. It was mostly about werewolves or vampires, nothing pertaining to Naturals or curses. Suddenly, the faint smell of blood caught his senses.

Marcello rushed out the door with an overwhelming and potentially irrational fear Astrid was in danger and concerned there may be a vampire who needed to be staked. He rushed out the door of his home and was at the scene of the attack in seconds, ready to act, but what he saw when he arrived caused him to hesitate.

He saw four beings in the alley: three males and one female. One of the males was lying on the ground, bloody and unresponsive; he was human. The woman was hysterically crying into the chest of one of the other men. They were both vampires, and there were a few drops of noticeable blood on her mouth.

The final man Marcello couldn't fully identify. He wasn't a vampire, but his smell wasn't human. He needed Astrid. She could identify any supernatural, even with her eyes closed.

He could feel the sadness and pain of the female vampire. His guess was she was young, still unsure of her strengths. It was probably an accidental kill. The assumption seemed even truer as he examined the faces of the two males. Neither of them looked shocked, just sad and disappointed, as if it had happened before. He could tell they were both worried.

Then, the male vampire looked straight at Marcello, who was standing out in the open in the middle of the alley. His original plan was to either save someone who was dying or kill a vampire. But his hesitation had left him motionless and vulnerable.

His concern wasn't that he thought he was in danger. His age allowed him to be much stronger than the young vampires he saw before him. However, they had seen him. So he knew their secret, and they were well aware that he knew.

With one quick glance, he saw the bar Astrid was meeting Carter at right down the street. He bolted there and slipped inside. He needed to find Astrid.

***

Once they were home and Marcello relayed his information to Astrid, the news didn't put her in a good mood. It made Astrid sad to know that the seemingly sweet vampire she saw at the bar had murdered someone. She felt bad for young vampires. It was critical they learn how to control their new strengths and urges, but it was a very difficult task that often caused many regretful mishaps.

Luckily, there was still hope for the young female vampire whose name she still didn't know. If young vampires showed remorse for killing, which the woman clearly did, then they could often overcome the darkness that followed becoming a vampire. Astrid was never able to overcome it during the short year she was a vampire before she was cursed. She wished every day she had tried harder.

She wondered sometimes if Marcello only stayed with her out of guilt. If he had never turned her, she would have never been cursed. Of course, if Astrid had learned some self-control, that would have helped too.

They sat at home, wondering if they should do anything about that young man being murdered. However, Astrid decided it was probably best if they just stuck to what they were doing. She was trying to slip into the group by befriending Carter, and if she could do that, she could hopefully find out their secrets. She needed to keep an eye on the female vampire because she couldn't have her killing everyone in town, but she wanted to give her a chance to learn self-control.

Hopefully, she wouldn't have to kill any more vampires before the current cycle of her curse ended. Unfortunately for Astrid, the odds were not in her favor for having these last few months be vampire-killing-free.

The next day, Astrid dawdled around the house most of the day. She bothered Marcello before he went to sleep, dusted a few things, and washed a dish or two. It was a pretty lazy day. Mostly, she just sat on the porch reading some of the books she saw sitting on Marcello's desk. It was hard for her to focus. She couldn't stop thinking about what Marcello had told her, but also a strange thought wouldn't leave her mind: Carter. There were so many questions she wanted to ask him, but also she couldn't stop thinking about his sharp jaw and his alluring eyes. His lips, which she had noticed, were pink and inviting. However, the thoughts were also sad. In a few months he wouldn't remember her. And even if she had a wonderful few months, it wouldn't be enough.

But maybe, just maybe, this was what she needed. Maybe the Natural who cursed her wanted her to fall in love with a vampire to break the curse. Or maybe she was just shit out of luck and would never be truly happy or content.

It was Tuesday, and she only had class on Monday, Wednesday, and Friday, so she was taking advantage of her day off. She went to the store and got a few food items for home. Carter had mentioned the night before that he also didn't have class. Astrid was tempted to call him, but they had planned to start working on their project that evening, so she resisted the urge.

By the time six p.m. rolled around, she started getting ready to head over to Carter's house. He had texted her earlier in the day. Her heart had done loops in her chest when she saw his text, but it subsided when she saw it was just his address. It was strange that she felt so strongly for someone she barely knew. Although they had talked some the night before, it wasn't anything of substance. But, for some reason, she felt like she knew him, and she really wanted to get to know him even more.

This time, she was smart; she drove over to Carter's house. Although it may have been nice to have him take her home, having her car there made it a safer situation, and she could leave anytime she wanted—or stay as late as she needed.

She arrived at Carter's house. It was much bigger than Astrid expected. He lived out in the middle of the woods with a gravel driveway similar to her house. It was obviously an old house, with green vines growing up and down every side. It was a tall two-story building with four windows on each level. He was at least a mile from his other neighbors. Although the population of the town was small, the area it covered was larger than smallest towns. That allowed people to have more land and more space. It was also a culturally rich small town, so the people were wealthy, and the houses were old but very nice and well kept.

Astrid hadn't realized how secluded and far off his home was, so she had misjudged how long it would take to get there. Unfortunately, it had made her late.

The time between her knocking on the door and him answering it was record-breaking. She would have been shocked if she didn't know he was a vampire, but she gave him a convincing surprised face and laugh. They greeted each other politely as new friends would. There was a moment where they both just stared at each other, Astrid wondering if she should hug him and he seemed to wonder the same thing. But she resisted and simply moved passed him into his home.

The place was all hardwood with high ceilings. No rugs to cover the floor, though, which she thought was weird. Not much furniture, either, to fill up the large home. She took a quick silent sniff to herself. Interesting, she thought. There was even food in the kitchen, which surprised Astrid—most vampires didn't bother to keep up the pretense since they got nothing from eating.

Unfortunately, she smelled something else when she sniffed: it was human blood. She could smell it in the basement. It caused Astrid to be worried, but she kept her demeanor calm and remained alert.

Carter shut the door, turned, and placed his hand on her shoulder, leading her into the dining area of the kitchen where his schoolwork was sprawled about. His touch sent a prickling pulse through her body, especially after she dared to look straight into his deep eyes, maybe never to return. His crisp smell surrounded her whole body.

She was almost dizzy from looking into his eyes, but her throat caught slightly and her mind returned to normal. She asked with a raspy voice, "Do you mind if I have a glass of water?"

"The water is broken right now," he awkwardly answered with a smile. "It acts up a lot. You know these old houses…" His uncomfortable smile grew larger.

That surprised her even more. Since he was smart enough to keep food in his house, she didn't know why there wouldn't be water. She considered that maybe it really was broken.

She wanted to laugh, but instead, she just shrugged and clear her throat as best and as awkwardly as she could.

"Oh!" he exclaimed. "I think I have bottles of water!" He ran almost too fast into the kitchen but slowed down as he walked back with a small bottle of water in his hand. Astrid took it and thanked him, once again catching his gaze. She smiled. She couldn't figure out what it was about him, but in all her lives, she had never so quickly and easily been caught up and distracted by someone. Especially a vampire.

"Shall we?" Carter asked as he motioned to dining room table. A very distinct wooden chair was placed at the head of the table, resembling a thrown. Naturally, this is where Carter sat. Astrid took a shallow breath to center herself and made her way to the end of the large ten-person table, and placed her small pink backpack on a chair.

After Astrid finally got past her smitten handicap and began thinking rational thoughts, they started working on their project. They developed a few ideas, but after about an hour, they put their schoolwork away and began to talk again like old friends.

Carter eventually mentioned they could move to the couch by the fireplace. Astrid agreed and Carter went over and made a fire. She watched him as he moved wood to the fireplace and light a match. It was hypnotizing. She realized they had abandoned any more schoolwork. Astrid felt a little uncomfortable just sitting without some kind of wine or tea to distract her hands. Her water bottle was long gone. She didn't eat a lot, but she liked having something in her hands like a drink or even a vape. She began to fidget a bit.

Suddenly, Carter reached over and gently took her hand into his. He began to examine it, his fingers caressing every point on her hand. He was so gentle and careful, as if he were examining the wings of a butterfly. She wondered if that was how he practiced touching people when he first turned. Vampires had to get used to their newfound strength when they were new. They often ripped off door handles and cabinets and crushed things they were trying to pick up. And most of the time, they hurt or killed a living being. They had to learn to be very careful.

They wouldn't mean to, but a newborn vampire's hug could break a person's spine, or a simple touch could break a bone. Whether they turned out to be a good vampire or not, they had to practice not breaking everything they touched. It was just one of the things young vampires had to learn to control.

That brought up another question, one she couldn't ask yet: how did he become a vampire?

She returned her mind to the moment, where he had moved from her hand to the soft, pale bottom side of her forearm, still touching ever so lightly. She knew he was looking at her veins. Vampires couldn't help it. It didn't mean he was going to bite her, but he couldn't resist seeing and feeling the blood flowing through her.

Like the crisp, airy smell that drew her to him, she, too, had a smell most vampires couldn't ignore. She wasn't a vampire, so she didn't drink blood, but she had heard from many sources that she smelled (and tasted) indescribably amazing.

Suddenly, his head lifted, and his eyes pierced through hers. He was looking deep into her eyes, searching for something.

"You should tell me a secret." His words were serious.

She thought about it for a moment, but she wasn't sure how to answer. Then, she realized what he was doing; he was trying to persuade her again. Maybe it was some final test to really see if she was a vampire or not, or to really see if she was completely evasive to persuasion.

Before she could answer, she heard the quick steps of something faster than a human running up the driveway. In a split second, the door opened. To her surprise, the male and female vampires entered the house.

Chapter 5

From the look on their faces, they weren't surprised Astrid was at the house. Carter didn't seem fazed when they walked through the door. Astrid wondered where the other guy was, the Natural.

The female vampire spoke first. Astrid was actually glad they were there. She wanted to learn their names—and she thought it might be easier to learn their secret if she befriended more than one of them.

"Hi, Astrid," she said in a very friendly way. "I'm Sara. And this is Grayson. Carter has told us all about you."

"Nice to meet you," Astrid said with a smile while she sat next to Carter on the couch.

"We're Carter's roommates," Sara mentioned. That explained why they just came walking into the house without knocking.

"I didn't know he lived with anyone," Astrid admitted.

The male vampire, who Astrid knew was Grayson, didn't say anything. He gave a faint smile and lightly touched Sara, as if to signal her out of the room. He looked nervous. Sara also had a slight look of concern, but she was far better at hiding her emotions than Carter and Grayson. Astrid had already picked up on that after last night when Sara showed almost no signs of distress sitting at the bar, even though she had just killed someone.

He gave Carter a look and motioned him upstairs while he and Sara made their way up. Carter excused himself for a moment and disappeared upstairs with the other two. Astrid heightened her senses, ready to hear anything they said upstairs. Unfortunately, what they said didn't make any sense.

***

"We can't find Duncan," Sara says.

"What do you mean you can't find Duncan?" Carter asked, seemly irritated.

"I told you this wasn't the time to be fooling around with that girl," He hissed out every word.

"I thought she could be of some use," Carter defended. "She might be something special. She can't be persuaded."

"And you thought now would be a good time to be curious about some random human?" Grayson sounded angry. "Sara is just now discovering her powers. We don't need a human liability."

"Guys, stop!" Sara begged. "If this isn't the time for anything, it's fighting. We are worried about Duncan."

"But we don't even know where it is!" Carter exclaimed. "If anyone could have found it, Duncan could have..."

There was a long pause. Astrid could almost feel the cool air that flowed around. She waited anxiously to see how everyone would react. She wasn't sure how long the three had been friends.

Grayson was the first to break the silence. "We need to find another wizard," he said after a short sigh.

Natural, Astrid thought to herself. She decided Duncan must have been the Natural she saw at the bar. And he had apparently fallen into the wrong hands. She wondered what the amulet was and what it could be used for.

"Once again, we need Duncan to find another wizard," Carter said.

Astrid heard him sit forcefully on a bed, as if giving up hope.

She decided to help.

She left Carter a note saying she needed to leave and she hoped everything was okay with his friends. She rushed back to the house to talk to Marcello. They knew some Naturals who might be willing to help.

When she made it home, frustrated by the excessive amount of time it took to drive instead of just running, Marcello was waiting for her on the porch.

"I made you a sandwich," he said as he held his creation in his hand. "I figured you would be hungry after eating dinner at a vampire's house. Did he have any food at all?" He smiled curiously.

Although Astrid wanted to hurry and find a Natural to help her new acquaintances, she decided to recount all the events from the evening with Marcello, leaving the mysterious conversation she overheard for last.

Marcello listened carefully to her every word, and his eyes widened as she recounted the conversation at the end of her story.

"Interesting," he said, almost to himself. "I'm curious about who this Alexa is."

They began to rack their minds as much as they could, trying to figure out who the mysterious, antagonizing person was.

Unfortunately, after a while of thinking, they realized they didn't have enough information to figure out who the woman was. They had never seen her, so they didn't know what she looked like—and they didn't know if she was a vampire, Natural, werewolf, or shape-shifter. Even if they had been able to think of someone with that name, they couldn't be certain it was her.

"We need to find a Natural who is willing to help," Astrid said, excited for the challenge.

Marcello, however, didn't seem so excited about her plan. He brought to light what Astrid hadn't really thought of yet. "What if these vampires aren't the good guys?" He encouraged Astrid to consider.

She had been so interested in the day-walking vampires and the mystery of the conversation she overheard, she didn't even wonder whether or not she was trying to help the right side.

"This Alexa could be simply fighting back because they did something to her first."

Astrid thought about it for a minute. Could those three be the bad guys?

Astrid was a good judge of character most of the time. She had to be since her purpose in life was to kill vampires. She had to be able to make the rational decision of whether or not the vampire she was about to kill was truly deserving of death.

She thought over the conversations she had with Carter, the innocent and sincere looks that fell across Sara's face, and the emotion and fear she felt when the three vampires were trying to figure out a way to save their Natural friend.

"I think if any vampire is willing to feel the fear they are feeling for their kidnapped friend," Astrid pointed out, "then they're worth helping."

Marcello paused, seeming to consider that. With the exception of Marcello being protective of Astrid, vampires often only felt the need to protect their own kind. They didn't connect well with other humans and supernatural, especially Naturals. Their friendship with the kidnapped Natural said something about their character. So, Marcello agreed to help.

They both thought of a few Naturals who might be willing to assist and decided on a plan of action. Asking a Natural to help in a potentially dangerous situation wasn't something that could be done over the phone. Also, the few Naturals that they knew may have a heart for a vampire like Marcello, but helping a vampire they don't know would be hard to convince. So they separated and darted off into the night to try and persuade someone to help.

Marcello only had time to visit two Naturals he knew before the sun started rising and he had to return home. He successfully spoke with both and, although they understood, neither would agree to help.

"Not our problem," one Natural had said.

"I love you, Marcello, but I don't get involved with vampires I don't know," said another.

Astrid was able to reach four Naturals before the late afternoon the next day. Unfortunately, all of them had similar answers: they didn't have enough information or any motive to help. That was what she was worried about. She didn't know anything about the amulet or Alexa, and she didn't know much about the three vampires she was trying to help. And even though another Natural was involved, and they were tempted, they just couldn't commit.

It was interesting because the only beings who ever remembered Astrid when her curse cycles ended were Naturals and, of course, Marcello. She didn't know why, but she didn't mind being remembered sometimes.

After failing to secretly get any help, Astrid was exhausted and hungry. Although she didn't need much sleep, the little she needed was almost mandatory for her to function. She was also angry about missing school, and it was only the second day of classes.

Unfortunately, she didn't have time to sleep or worry about class. It was almost dark, and she needed to try and find Duncan. She hoped that if no one knew she was helping, she could find him and save him without raising any concerns.

She decided to start at Carter's house. She assumed they would be off looking for Duncan or the amulet, so she could explore the house and maybe find a clue to point her in the right direction.

She ate a quick meal and changed out of her clothes from the day before. She put on a fitted white polo with tight black jeans.

She drove to the house, but when she got there, her senses heightened, and she felt very uneasy. Everything was off: the smell, the taste in the air, even the outside of the house itself seemed eerier. She looked around and found a small stick on the ground. She picked it up and stashed it under her shirt sleeve just in case.

A strong smell of crisp, sweet vampire blood filled the air when she stepped out of the car. The door to the house was opened a little, and she heard faint sounds of pain coming from inside, along with an obvious smell of more than just three vampires in the house.

She was sure they'd heard her coming. The faint whispers and stillness from inside the house proved it. She walked up to the door, trying to keep a normal persona by managing a simple hum, but ready to attack at any moment.

At the door, she called out Carter's name as she gently knocked. She lightly pushed open the heavy dark wooden door as she called out. "Hello…? Anyone home?"

She walked toward the smell of blood in the living room, hearing in detail the sound of severe pain.

"Hey, Carter, are you here? The door was open." She finally saw the blood she smelled, and it was dripping out of Carter and Grayson, who were wounded on the floor. Both had large stakes jabbed through them in multiple places. Wooden stakes were a weakness of vampires. Even if an attacker didn't manage to stake a vampire through the heart to kill them, a wooden stake anywhere in their bodies would impair them, causing severe pain.

Sara was unconscious on the floor.

Astrid paused when she saw them, attempting to act more shocked than she felt since she was still trying to imitate a human. The distinct wooden chair that Astrid had noticed visiting the night before was in pieces, presumably in Carter and Grayson's arms and legs.

"Get out!" Carter shouted in agony on the floor, almost trying to get up to protect her and lead her out the door.

Before she had a chance to react again, a man appeared a few feet beside her. He was a vampire. She tried to act startled, although she had heard him coming. She turned to face him as she attempted a look of shock on her face.

He was a tall vampire, and he had a look of hunger in his eyes. Excitement flared in hers; she was ready for a fight.

At the same time that Carter desperately screamed "No!" from the floor, the tall vampire was on her, arms wrapped around her body, teeth millimeters from piercing through her seemingly innocent neck. What stopped him was the stake

Astrid had up her sleeve. She jabbed it through his quickly dying heart and pulled back as the red vampire blood quickly turned to ash on the stake.

She stepped back and looked into his eyes as the hunger turned to confusion and finally to pure white. His whole body began to change, losing all color and size, shriveling up into a white pile of ash as all vampires did when they died.

The shock and awe on Carter and Grayson's face were undeniably noticeable; they could have never expected what had just happened. They were so confused they didn't even think to warn Astrid there were a lot more vampires in the house. But it didn't matter. She already knew there were more, and she was more than ready to fight. She could hear and smell as they stepped out of the shadows of the house, ready to avenge the vampire she had just killed.

With the wooden stake still in her hands, in one swift wave, they charged her. The first vampire to make it to her reached for Astrid, but with her hunter strength, she grabbed his shoulders and threw him into two others that were running at her. They went flying across the room while she spun and kicked another's legs out from under them and jabbed the stake into their heart while still in mid-air and guided them to the ground. Dust began to fill the air as she left her stake on the ground.

Astrid quickly stood up, then leaped and landed next to Carter. She mouthed "Sorry" and ripped one stake from each leg. He screamed, but quickly his face went back to shock as she ran toward two other vampires and, with a wooden stake in each hand, she stabbed them both in the heart. More ash filled the air.

Now, the one she had thrown and the two who had been hit were running toward her. She lifted the two stakes from the ash and threw them at two of the vampires running toward her. They both turned instantly to dust.

The last of the six who had originally attacked her had stopped and was in shock at the sight of all his mates gone. But his face changed to rage and he ran at Astrid. She ran toward him with the same speed, but bent down and slid over to the Grayson. This time she looked at him and mouthed "So sorry" and ripped the stake that was in his arm. He flinched but didn't make a noise, just continued to watch.

The vampire who she had dodge was now running toward her while she looked in the other direction. But he didn't stand a chance. She turned around at the perfect moment and all that was left was dust.

In the same short split-second amount of time it took for them to attack, she had killed them. She stabbed six vampires in the heart, never missing.

They never had a chance.

Only seconds later, the seventh and final vampire in the house made her stand. She was obviously the leader. She was older and had a calm air that surrounded her. Astrid was tempted to ask how old she was, but instead, she stood tall, her white shirt covered in fresh splatters of vampire ash.

Astrid dropped her stake to the ground, faced her opponent, and looked her square in the eyes with a smug smile. She didn't need weapons to kill a vampire.

The older woman vampire gave her an equally challenging smile, changed her stance, and charged at Astrid at full speed, almost too fast for Carter and Grayson to see. But Astrid could. She was a pro at fighting older vampires. She was faster than most.

And she was faster than that vampire.

Astrid dodged the attack, and when the female vampire turned to her, ready to attack again, Astrid struck. She rammed her fist straight through the vampire's chest, grabbed onto her heart, and ripped it clean from her.

The female vampire stood for a second, her face filled with shock and pain. Then, Astrid once again watched as the color and life slowly drifted from a vampire's body, turning to nothing but a white pile of ash.

Chapter 6

The words "shock" and "awe" were no way to describe the looks on Carter and Grayson's faces; they were stunned and completely speechless. All the pain they were feeling drifted away for a few brief moments as they processed what had just unfolded around them.

Astrid was motionless, standing in the same position with a pile of white ash in her hand that took the place of the dead vampire's heart. Her muscles were tense, and her breath was sharp and deep. She began to close her eyes and compose herself.

Astrid was weak from a lack of food and sleep. As she began to come down from her heightened hunter sense, she began to feel light-headed. She let out a faint giggle as she fumbled to find something to hold herself up. That was not how she wanted the fight to end. She hated feeling helpless.

She wanted to run out of the door and into her house, where Marcello probably was, waiting for her to return. She had never told him she was going over there. To him, she could still be looking for a Natural or getting a drink at a bar.

As she fell to the ground, she looked in the direction of Carter and Grayson, the room spinning around her. She gave a small uncomfortable smile and hit the floor hard. A streak of curse words raged through her mind as she unwillingly closed her eyes and lost all consciousness.

***

Astrid jolted from the place she was lying, fully aware of what had just happened. In an instant, she processed her surroundings.

She was on the red leather couch in Carter's living room, the same one she had tried to hold herself up on before she passed out. The vampires weren't in the room, but stakes lay sprawled out on the ground along with grey ash.

It was daylight but still early in the morning, though. Marcello was probably beside himself worrying about her last night. She would need to go see him soon or he probably wouldn't sleep all day. Like her, vampires needed their sleep.

She heard footsteps upstairs, and out of the corner of her eye, she saw a slow, lingering movement.

She whipped her head to the side to see who was spying on her: it was the Natural, who she knew was named Duncan. As she was about to stand up to greet him, she felt something like a hammer hit her head, and she was out again in an instant.

***

This time, Astrid woke up more slowly, irritated. It was late morning; a couple hours had passed. She touched her head—no bump or bruise. Although she healed quickly, there should have been at least a small mark left.

A small wave of anger crept through her body; Duncan had done some kind of spell on her. Since she was cursed, she was very sensitive about Naturals using their magic on her, especially in a negative way. All she had done was woken up, and he attacked her.

This time, the movement to her side was Carter. She glared at him; she wasn't happy about Duncan knocking her out.

"He was worried," Carter said as he sensed her anger. "He said you started to move, and you looked like you woke up in such a panic, he thought you might attack him."

"I was going to walk over and shake his hand," Astrid said through gritted teeth. "Introduce myself." This time, Astrid did stand up, and she started to make her way to the door.

"Where are you going?" Carter asked, condescendingly.

"I'm leaving," she hissed. "Isn't that obvious?" Astrid wasn't playing games anymore. The spell from Duncan had set her over the edge. She had saved their lives, and they repaid her by having a Natural attack her. It was not settling well.

Since Astrid was leaving at a normal human speed, Carter flashed to the door before her, bolting the lock.

"No, you're not," he ordered. "We need to talk. Now."

Astrid looked at him for a moment and wished he still had one of those stakes resting in his side to cause him some pain. Instead, in one swift move of her arm, she hit him so hard he flew into the wall behind him. With the same speed, she kicked down the heavy, wooden door, heard the hurried sound of footsteps coming down the stairs, and looked straight into Carter's eyes.

"Don't ever tell me what to do." And then she was gone, but she felt the eyes of the other three who had witnessed the event as she walked out the door.

***

By the time Marcello woke, Astrid had time to eat, sleep, and email all of her professors to apologize for missing class. All of them sent back a similar email, as if they had written it together, stating "attendance was not mandatory, but strongly recommended." She had also changed out of her dusty clothes and was wearing black gym pants and a fitted, gray shirt.

The one thing Astrid had not had time to do was calm down. She had slept, but her dreams were not relaxing. She needed to vent to Marcello before she could do that.

He woke to find her sitting on the second-floor balcony, watching the faint dark colors fade away into the sunset, replaced by the night sky. He was relieved. Since she hadn't come home the night before, Marcello was very worried. She'd woken him up for a brief moment when she returned earlier in the day, so he knew she was there. Still, it was a relief for him to see her sitting outside when he awoke.

Astrid had heard Marcello stirring inside, but she waited to talk to him until he was fully awake and ready to join her outside. The first thing Marcello often did when he woke up was eat. They had a stash of blood bags in the basement fridge so Marcello did not have to feed off of humans. All of the blood in the bags was Astrid's.

She was the ultimate vampire blood source, which had more than once caused trouble for her. Since she was a hunter, her wounds healed quickly, and her blood replenished even faster. So she frequently filled blood bags for Marcello to feed on. His diet consisted of almost 100 percent her blood, and he liked it.

Astrid's blood smelled, and tasted, unusually amazing to vampires. She blamed it on being a hunter, with the smell attracting vampires, which helped in her hunts.

A few minutes later, after Marcello had fed, he joined her on the porch, giving her a sweet touch on the shoulder and a smile that said, "I'm glad you're okay."

"So," he said, "you woke me up to tell me you were alive, but what happened? Where were you last night?"

Astrid told her story, which started with her search for a Natural who could help and ended with her dramatic exit from Carter's house. At some points, Marcello had a look of concern on his face, while at other points, a look of pride and curiosity. He loved many qualities about Astrid, and her spunk was definitely one of them.

"To sum things up," Astrid started, "Duncan is fine—and I kind of hate him. I killed seven vampires last night while blowing my cover and found out that the three vampires are definitely on someone's bad side."

"So you had a pretty good night," Marcello teased.

She played along: "Eh, the fighting was fun, but the passing out and spell attacks were not so fun."

"Did they come see you today while I was asleep?" Marcello asked.

"No, they don't know where I live," Astrid admitted. "But it won't take them too long to figure it out. I'm sure they're dying to know everything: who I am, what I am, blah, blah, blah."

"This could work to our advantage," Marcello said while Astrid gave him a confused look. "You can tell them bits about yourself and your life in return for information about their situation."

Astrid wasn't convinced.

"I don't know." She sighed. "After last night, I'm not sure I really want to get involved. I mean, I already missed a whole day of school, and it's only the second day of class!"

"Unfortunately, Astrid, you may not have much of a choice," Marcello regretfully admitted. "They know you're strong. They've seen you fight. Which means they're probably going to ask you for help at some point, whether we like it or not."

Astrid knew what Marcello was talking about. It had happened a few times before. Astrid had blown her cover by helping someone or not being careful enough. Once she did that, people started asking for help. Even though they didn't know anything about her, they knew she was strong. Once people knew she was a fighter, they wanted her on their side—and they'd bug her until she caved.

Although Astrid knew that was true, she decided to wait until they came to her. She didn't want to seem too curious about their situation, and she wanted to have the upper hand.

Astrid fell asleep early, shortly after she and Marcello had talked. But around 3:00 a.m., there was a faint knock at the door.

She cautiously got ready to entertain her unexpected guests and listened closely as Marcello answered the door. "What an unexpected surprise," she heard Marcello say sarcastically downstairs; although, if someone didn't know any better, his subtle sarcasm could almost seem sincere.

"We need to speak to Astrid," Carter demanded. The whole crew had shown up to be part of the discussion: Sara, Duncan, Carter, and Grayson. "I think you know why we're here."

Just as Marcello was about to invite the four inside, Astrid appeared. She was dressed in long tight jeans and a loose white peasant shirt that was revealing a little too much. Her hair was down and loose. She had obviously just woken up.

She began to fix her hair into a loose bun on her head, yawning a little. "It's kind of late to be making house calls, don't you think?" Astrid asked with a devious smile. None of the four were impressed with her humor, although a slight smile crept onto Carter's face. "I guess you all can come inside. I'll make some tea," she said, knowing only she and potentially Duncan would drink any of it.

Astrid went into the kitchen and yawned sleepily as she placed the kettle on the stove; she had school in a few hours, and she clearly wasn't going to go back to bed. Marcello lead the four guests into the living room and offered them a seat on his outdated couch.

"We're not here to play games," Grayson insisted as he refused the seat Marcello offered him in the living room. That was the first time he had spoken. Astrid heard him in the kitchen. His voice was deep and smooth; one of those voices that can be heard reverberating through the whole house. "We want to know what you're doing here." He wasn't asking—he was ordering.

Astrid walked into the room, leaned against the door frame between the kitchen and living room, and rubbed her eyes as she gave another sleepy yawn. "Listen," she began, "it's 3:00 in the morning, I have class in a few hours, and I'm exhausted. So, I'll give you the shorthand story. But, in return, I want to know why there was a horde of vampires at your house last night trying to kill you."

"You tell us your side of the story, and maybe we will tell you ours," Grayson said with a scowl across his face.

Astrid stood taller, stiffer, and said in a stern voice, looking right into Grayson's eyes, "Oh, you will tell me your side of the story, even if I have to force it out of you."

Marcello quickly walked over to Astrid and gave her a gentle squeeze on the shoulder to calm her down. Once again, something was telling her what to do and she didn't like it. She looked at Marcello, her face hard and cold; she gave a quick, short sigh and cast a swift glance at all of their faces: Grayson seemed angry, and Carter looked serious. Duncan had a suspicious look, one Astrid didn't trust, and Sara looked sad but sweet and gentle. Astrid had the urge to protect her, to keep her safe. If it wasn't for Sara's sweet smile, she may have not wanted to help them as much.

"So, here's the short version," Astrid began, speaking almost sarcastically. But, before she could start telling her story, they all heard another knock at the door.

Chapter 7

"Are you expecting someone else?" Carter asked suspiciously.

"No, you were our only unexpected guests," Astrid shot back. "I have no idea who this could be." Astrid moved slightly to her left and opened and closed a small in table near her where a few wooden stakes were hidden and placed one up her sleeve and another around her waist; one could never have too many wooden stakes handy. Carter and Sara noticed and gave suspicious frowns. "What?" Astrid asked as she walked over to the window by the door.

Grayson made his way quietly over to the door and peeked out the window. He faintly muttered, "Shit," but the voices outside spoke before he could elaborate.

"We're looking for the girl." A deep-voiced female spoke from outside.

Astrid headed over to the window to get a quick glance. From what she could see and smell, there were at least ten vampires outside. No other supernatural were out there, which was a good thing. It was always best to only have to fight one type of supernatural at a time. Plus, they had a Natural in-house, whom Astrid regretfully had learned knew how to use his powers.

"What girl do you think they are talking about?" Astrid asked curiously as she turned back to her first set of uninvited guests. She wasn't really nervous, but she didn't want a fight at her house.

"Well," Carter started, "this is your house, so I'm guessing they're looking for you." Lies glittered behind his eyes.

"Send out the young vampire girl now and no one gets hurt," the female vampire from outside said.

Astrid gave Carter a smile as he rolled his eyes. "Yeah, I'm pretty sure they're not after me," she said as she looked over at Sara.

"Send out the hunter as well," the female vampire spoke again. "They both have to pay for their crimes."

It was Astrid's turn to roll her eyes. She had killed a handful of vampires the previous night, so it wasn't too shocking she had gotten on their hit list. "What did you do to piss these lunatics off?" Astrid said almost jokingly to Sara. "I mean, it's probably pretty obvious why they might not be a fan of me. But you guys? You must have done something bad."

Sara put her head down and stuttered a bit, unsure of how to answer Astrid's question.

"It doesn't matter what she did," Grayson said as he stepped in front of Sara, as if to protect her from Astrid's intense gaze. "And I assure you, these vampires are not lunatics; they're organized and powerful."

"Well, they're lunatics for coming to my house expecting to win a fight," Astrid said under her breath as she looked out the window again. The vampires outside were getting ready for something, and it wasn't good.

She couldn't hear what they were saying. Curse their quiet vampire voices, Astrid thought to herself. She smelled gasoline and could see the matches in most of their hands, ready to light. "Oh, hell no!" Astrid shouted. "They're going to burn down my house!"

She glanced over at Sara while she decided what she was going to do. Grayson and Carter took this as a sign that Astrid was planning on giving Sara to the vampires outside.

"No!" demanded Carter. "We're not giving her over to them, even if we have to fight you and them."

"Who said anything about giving her up?" Astrid asked, a confused look in her eyes. "We're gonna kick some ass because I'm not having my house burnt down, especially when I have no idea why. Next time you have vengeful vampires following you, don't come to visit me."

"You were the one who got involved," Carter said shyly, as if he really didn't mean it.

"Ok," she laughed. "Next time I won't save your lives."

In one swift move of her arm, Astrid had a stake in each hand. It surprised the three young vampires inside, but Marcello walked right up to Astrid, ready to fight.

"How many are out there?" Marcello asked in a calm voice.

Astrid took a deep breath and closed her eyes. She attuned her senses to the world around her. In a mere second, Astrid could smell each individual creature outside the window, her ears capturing every sound.

"At least ten," Astrid answered as she opened her eyes and looked around the room. "I think we can take them." Astrid got really close to Marcello and whispered her recently-thought-up plan into his ear, too quiet for anyone inside or outside to hear.

"What are you doing?" Grayson asked with his voice raised. "Whatever it is, you're not doing it without us."

"Oh, hush," Astrid said, giving him a disapproving look. "We don't need your help. Stay inside. Trust me," she said calmly as she gave Sara a reassuring look. "Let us protect you. There's a hatch in the closet that leads to a space in the basement for Marcello in case something was to happen to the house. Go in there."

The three vampires and Duncan stood silently while they looked cautiously at each other. They seemed unsure about what to do or who to trust. Astrid just shrugged and disappeared instantly; she was more worried about her house being burnt down.

Marcello made his way out of the front door, not even looking or caring where the stowaways in the house were planning on going. He exited tentatively, sticking both hands out of the front door to signify he was unarmed as he pushed the rest of his body through.

"Where's the girl?" demanded a small redheaded female vampire. She was clearly not in the mood for chatting.

"Now, listen," Marcello started, "can we talk for a second?"

"There's nowhere for you to go," the female vampire said once again, still seeming uninterested. "We have the house surrounded."

"I know," Marcello said calmly. "I just want to talk for a minute." As Marcello finished that last sentence, Astrid began the attack while the four stowaways inside watched from the windows.

Astrid silently made her way outside. She struck quickly, quietly staking the vampires in the back of the house first, then making her way to the front in a matter of milliseconds. She wasn't playing around. Not one of them saw her coming. It happened too fast.

No human could see her attack. Even Duncan, who was a Natural, all but blinked twice, and the vampires outside were killed.

All the gasoline cans fell to the ground at almost the same time.

She was a silent hunter, and she was skilled at her art. She never missed, never hesitated, and always accomplished her goal. She and Marcello had faltered before. But after so many years of fighting, Astrid was almost unstoppable.

She paused for a brief moment as she silently stood behind the female vampire; she gave her a second to see the dead bodies quickly turning to white ash all around her. And right as the female vampire drew a scowl on her face and began to turn toward the figure behind her, Astrid snapped her neck. She wasn't ready to kill the vampire yet. She wanted to talk first. Snapping a vampire's neck wouldn't kill them, just render them unconscious for a couple hours. Unfortunately, her house "guests" didn't approve of her idea.

"What are you doing?" shouted Carter from the front steps. He and the other three from inside had made their way to the front door's steps, while Marcello was now swiftly by Astrid's side.

"I'd like to talk to this one," Astrid said, looking down as Marcello carefully lifted the sleeping body off the ground.

"No! You can't do that!" Carter exclaimed. "We have to kill her before it's too late."

"You do realize," Astrid began, "that you're standing on my front steps, and this vampire is in my front lawn, and I just knocked her out? What part of this do you think you have control over exactly?"

"This woman is dangerous," Grayson said, speaking more calmly than before. "If we don't kill her now, we may not have another chance."

"Sweetheart, how do we know you four aren't dangerous?" Astrid asked condescendingly. But before they could answer, Marcello and she both let out an exaggerated laugh and made it very clear they did not believe those four were a threat.

As they brought the female vampire inside, amidst the protests of their guests, Astrid became increasingly aware of Duncan, who wasn't saying anything. She wasn't scared of him, but she knew he had more power than she did, even though she was such a strong fighter. She wondered how he had escaped his capture. She began to keep a close eye on him, as he did on her, while he simply glanced around the room, thinking. She started to wonder how well they were going to get along since he was a Natural.

"Listen, you don't understand," Carter protested as Marcello laid the female vampire onto the couch. They started to get frantic as they tried to convince Marcello and Astrid to kill the unconscious woman. All the while, Sara stood silently behind Grayson, always watching but never speaking.

"Then why don't you tell us what's going on?" Astrid said, interrupting Carter and Grayson's protests.

They stood silent for a minute while they looked at each other.

"You wouldn't get it," Duncan said, finally adding to the conversation. "You haven't been here the past few months."

"Besides, we don't even know who or what you are," Grayson interjected.

Marcello and Astrid exchanged a look.

"I'm a vampire hunter," Astrid said blatantly. She wasn't going to delve into all her secrets or explain her curse, but she decided to at least give them a little background on herself. "Marcello and I were friends before he was turned and before I became a hunter. We've been fighting together on and off for… two thousand years or so."

Everyone in the room fell silent. Saying the words "vampire hunter" around a group of vampires was always a risk. Astrid also realized they were probably a little confused by her and Marcello's relationship.

"We don't just go around murdering every vampire we see," Astrid said as the three vampires gave a faint, awkward smile of relief.

"Although, when in doubt, killing is normally our first reaction," Marcello said with a smile.

The rest of the room was not amused.

"We're just trying to keep people safe," Astrid said with a serious tone in her voice. "Humans have no defense against vampires. Killing the malicious ones and stopping some of the violent families from going on massacres is our way of giving humans an advantage."

Sometimes, vampires joined together in large groups, often called families. They got that name not because the vampires were related by birth but because they were related by blood. Most of the time, those groups had two or three older vampires who created a generation of younger vampires, who then created another generation, and so forth and so on. They often lived together.

The families could be all sorts of sizes with all sorts of common mannerisms; some families were known for killing, while others were known for being peaceful. Astrid had made it a habit of getting rid of the violent families. It was often a difficult task because she had to make sure she killed every single one of them. Those who lived together for a long time and were related by blood became connected. They could feel each other's pain and joy; kill one, and all the others would know they died—and how it happened.

In order to kill a family and not face repercussions, Astrid had to kill all of them quickly; that way, her face and name died with them. Her curse was already the result of someone taking revenge. She didn't want anyone else holding a grudge against her.

However, Astrid was well known. Younger vampires did not know her by her face or her name. They knew her by her actions as a never-aging vampire hunter who was ruthless and unstoppable.

At one time, she had tried to kill all of the vampires alive. She didn't waste her time figuring out the difference between the nice ones and the bad ones; she killed them all, except Marcello. Although, it was unspoken, but known, that once she had killed them all, Marcello would have to die as well.

She thought she could end her curse if all the vampires were dead; she was desperate to be free. But it broke her heart to look into the eyes of kind and gentle vampires as she jabbed a stake through their hearts.

Eventually, she realized it was impossible to kill them all. Once she had killed so many that she thought she was almost done, her curse cycle would end and when she regained her memory sixteen years later Marcello would inform her of another ten or fifteen families that had appeared and he couldn't fight on his own. So, after a few hundred years of brutally killing, she stopped. Marcello and she came up with a new plan to protect the humans and only hunt down the vampires who deserved it. All the while, Astrid was left scarred by all the innocent vampires she had slaughtered.

But that night, Astrid and Marcello stood before their newfound "friends" while both sides tried to decide whether or not to trust one another.

Suddenly, Sara broke her silence.

"I killed someone," Sara said, her head down low as her eyes stared at the floor. She slowly lifted her gaze to meet Astrid's, whose eyes carried no judgment. "I didn't mean to…"

Although Grayson kept a stern barrier between her and Sara, Astrid moved closer to Sara, trying to give her a comforting glance. "Tell me what happened," Astrid said gently, "and maybe we can find a way to help."

And so Sara began to tell the story of her accidental kill.

Chapter 8

Sara lay curled up on the damp ground in the middle of the woods on a cold night. She was beginning to change.

Humans didn't have a choice in the matter of becoming a vampire; if a vampire wanted them to turn, they were going to turn. To ignite the change was simple, but it was a painful process.

In order to change, a human must be bitten by a vampire, therefore releasing that vampire's venom into their system. The venom was what made a vampire's bite so pleasurable to some. But it could also be painful. If someone accepted a bite willingly, the venom would flow through their system like a shot of heroin. But if they resisted, it felt like pure fire in their veins; however, no matter whether a human resisted or not, during the change, the venom felt like fire. The change could take a few hours or, in some rare cases, a few days.

Once the transformation began, so did the pain. Fire burned through their system as the body morphed its composition to that of a vampire. Everything shifted, even their minds. There was nothing that could be done to stop it.

Sometimes, the human body couldn't handle it, and they simply died in the process. But most made it through the transformation as completely different beings.

Sara was just beginning her transformation. She had been bitten a few hours earlier and had woken up alone in the woods. She lay curled on the ground as tears streamed down her face.

She began to convulse on the ground, her body in too much pain to even cry; unorganized grunts and moans of pain began as the fire pulsed through her body, under her skin, behind her eyes. Everywhere.

She couldn't blink, couldn't see, and couldn't escape the agony. All she could think about was the pain and the fear. She wished Grayson or Carter was there to make her feel safe. She remembered the bite. She remembered the face of the monster who had attacked her. She barely knew the man and didn't know why he had chosen her for such horrific torture. She struggled to breathe while she grasped desperately at the ground with her hands. She pulled up dirt and roots but never caught hold of anything for comfort.

But Sara was lucky. Her change was quick, only lasting a few minutes.

She lay motionless on the ground, suddenly feeling no pain. She wondered where it had all gone. Surprisingly, she felt good, great even. Instead of pain, energy and life pulsed through her body. She let out a moan of pleasure. The pain was gone, and she felt like she was radiating, like she was glowing with energy. She started to hear things walking all around her, even the soft sound of bugs crawling at her feet. Her eyes not only adjusted to the dark, but she could see everything, not as if it were day, but as if everything glowed as it produced its own light that she could see in the dark.

It was beautiful and amazing, and she truly felt like she could fly.

Then, she heard the faint footsteps of what she would learn was a vampire, and he appeared—the one who had turned her.

Her light, airy feeling of energy disappeared, and a dark haze enveloped her. She felt anger like she had never felt before, as if it consumed her whole body. Her breathing became erratic. She was still radiating, but it was a fiery red feeling of rage that oozed from every pore. Her thoughts whirled around in her mind, unable to be controlled. She stared at him straight in his eyes as he whispered, "Hello, beautiful. Welcome to the family," with a soft smile across his face.

And she killed him. In a mere fraction of a second, she stood, face-to-face with her maker. She sent her hand straight into his chest, gripped tightly around his beating heart, and ripped it straight out, watching as he turned into a pile of white ash.

Before she could feel the joy of her kill, a new wave of emotion constricted her every move; she felt pure, piercing guilt. She had just killed someone.

In an instant, she thought of the man she had killed and what he had done to her, and the rage once again flashed through her body. She fell to the ground, incapable of handling the quick-changing, unbearable emotions; each one enveloped her entire body and controlled her every action.

She lay there silently, feeling the cool earth beneath her smooth hands. The ground felt different, amazing. She felt every groove, smelled every smell, and could even sense the vibrations as the earth moved beneath her body.

She took a deep breath as she relished in that one moment of calm, trying to find a way to hold onto it so the emotions would stop. She remembered what Grayson had told her; when he had changed, the emotions were incapacitating. But when he started to feel still and calm, he found ways to remember that feeling so he could bring it back when he needed it.

Sara closed her eyes. She gave the moment, her calm feeling, a name: serenity. She gave it a taste: crisp. She visualized the dark browns, the crunching leaves, the soft vibrations beneath; they swirled together in her mind, all wrapped together with their new taste and name. She held onto it. That was her peace. Her serenity. She lost herself in thought, fell peacefully to the ground, and drifted into relaxation. She wasn't asleep but reveling in the calm feeling.

She wasn't sure how long it had been (seconds, minutes, hours), but she heard the faint but fast sounds of footsteps headed toward. She opened her eyes quickly and sat up on high alert, no longer calm and serene.

"Sara! Are you okay?" Carter shouted above her, reaching to try to wake her. She was startled. She stood up quickly and moved to get away. But she moved much faster than expected, and she slammed into a tree. Although she knew she would heal, it didn't take away the pain she currently felt. She reached for her head as a few tears fell from her eyes.

Carter didn't move toward her. He lowered his body to a crouch and lifted his hands, as if to show her he meant no harm. He spoke softly, with a calm but serious face. "Sara, it's okay. It's just me, Carter."

She looked at him, the pain from the tree diminishing. So many emotions rushed through her mind and body, and all she could do was cover her ears and take deep breaths.

"Hey," Carter whispered calmly with a kind smile across his face. Although he hid it well, he was shocked. He never expected to find her like this. He never expected Sara to become a vampire. But he was running out of time. "It's okay. Listen, Sara, we have to go. The sun is coming up soon. We need to get you to a safe place." She looked up at him cautiously, realizing the danger she was in. "I know you're confused, and there's a lot going through your mind right now. But we have to go."

He reached out his hand slowly, but not slowly enough. Sara reacted defensively. She tensed her body, ready to fight. As her senses heightened, she was caught off guard; for the first time, her fangs grew, jutting out of her gums like molten knives. She screamed; it always hurt the first time. Carter, however, took the distraction to his advantage. He ran to her, wrapped her tight in his arms, and whispered calm phrases as Sara fought like a wild animal to get free.

A newly created vampire was like a feral baby animal, nearly uncontrollable and unpredictable. Most would come to their senses in a few hours. As Carter held on tight to his struggling friend, he hoped she wouldn't be one of the unlucky newborns who take days to regain control.

Sara continued to scramble to get free, but Carter held tight. He wasn't worried about her overtaking him; he was much older than she was, and much stronger, and she had no combat training yet. But the sun was lurking behind the horizon as it began its ascent to slither its way into the sky. He needed to get her home fast.

But just as he was about to snap her neck to render her unconscious for her own good, she began to cry. She wrapped her arms around Carter and mumbled into his shoulder, "Please, get me out of here."

In one swoop, he lifted her off the ground and ran as fast as he could to his home, with the sun crawling up his back.

***

As it turned out, the four of them living together was a new development, and Marcello and Astrid were interested in finding out. It had only happened a days earlier when Sara was turned. She needed to be watched almost constantly, so she moved in with Carter, Grayson, and Duncan.

Carter and Grayson were the only two living together at first. Grayson was Carter's creator. They didn't delve into the details, but Carter was approximately one hundred years old, while Grayson was around two hundred.

Duncan, however, a few months before, moved into the house next, after his house was burned down by a group of angry werewolves working for a "bad witch," as they put it. That was another story they didn't delve into, but they did add that they'd "handled the situation," indicating the Natural was dead.

That was the moment that Astrid realized her newfound friends had a knack for getting into trouble, which was interesting, considering she had come to town to stay out of trouble.

"That's all good to know," Astrid said with a slightly condescending tone, "but could you explicitly tell us why all these vampires are after you?"

"I think that's pretty obvious," Duncan said, looking Astrid right in the eyes. "Sara killed a member of a vampire family, and now they want her dead. I'm not even a vampire, and I knew that."

Astrid was tempted to call him out on not even knowing what his own kind was called. He threw around the word "witch" like it was nothing. She bet he even called himself a wizard. She shuddered at that thought; what a stupid name. But, she decided not to pick on the lonely little Natural who had probably never had a true teacher to call him by his actual name.

"Well, Duncan," Astrid said, ready to pick a fight. "Why don't you tell us how to get to the place where this family lives? Not only were you kidnapped and probably brought there, but you can use a locator spell to find the location. And, by the way, how exactly did you escape from them in the first place?"

Duncan was taken aback. He looked around at all the people in the room. Apparently, no one had really pestered him on how he escaped. They had just accepted he was free, and that was good enough. A strange look of fear crept over his face, remembering the details of his escape.

"They sort of just let me go," he said to himself. "I can't exactly remember."

Astrid and Marcello weren't buying it. The look on his face had too much to say.

"Why don't you tell us exactly what happened, and you'd better hurry. I'm not sure how much longer this one is going to be unconscious," Astrid said, motioning to the female vampire resting on her couch.

And so he did.

Chapter 9

It was close to dark a few days prior, and Duncan was beginning to leave downtown Blessings and return home. He almost always left enough time between sunset and dark to make it home, except he got caught up rummaging through a new section of history books in the bookshop downtown. He had decided to walk to the store, so it would be at least thirty minutes before he made it home; it would definitely be dark before he made it back.

That day, however, Duncan wasn't worried about being alone in the dark. Although he had been in some intense and dangerous situations in the past year, especially ones that involved creatures that came out at night, it had been a rather calm few weeks. He wasn't hunting through his spell books or magic history books looking for something to kill a demon, or solve a mystery, or save a friend. He had free time to do what he wanted and relax.

The only unusual thing to happen recently was his friend, Sara, becoming a vampire. It hadn't been a facile time calming her down and handling her almost uncontrollable nature. It had only been a few days, but she had good mentors to help her.

At first, they were worried. No one knew why the unnamed, unknown vampire had chosen Sara to be changed. And after her rage-filled transformation, she had killed him. They were concerned someone would be missing the dead vampire.

But, after a few days of no one coming to avenge his death, everyone relaxed. Vampires were not the type to hold off on revenge, although Carter and Grayson still kept a close eye on Sara, just in case.

Duncan wasn't worried, though. He'd become accustomed to things going bump in the dark, and he was convinced things would stay normal for a while.

He walked home peacefully, feeling the cool breeze on his skin and the nature all around him. It had been a while since he was that happy. Ever since he'd lost his house and his mother, an ominous cloud had followed him around that threatened to turn him dark. His mother didn't get to teach him much before she died, but she made one thing clear: being overwhelmed with negative emotions could turn him *dark*.

Using magic through hate and sadness was a wicked and consuming magic. She never wanted him to lose sight of goodness.

He had been worried, and so had his friends, that he might lose himself after he lost everything else. But his friends stood by his side, opening their home and hearts to him. Those days, he saw light in almost anything, except that girl.

He had only seen Astrid once, at school, but he didn't like her. He felt something around her, something he couldn't explain. But whatever it was, it was dark. It surrounded every inch of her, and it was permanent. It had been there for a while, and she wasn't a stranger to darkness. And that actually scared him.

He wasn't thinking of her then, though, just walking back home to his friends, enjoying the calm night. He wasn't thinking or focusing on anything. His mind was wandering. That was why he never heard or felt them coming. One minute he was walking and daydreaming of good things, and the next, he felt a sharp pain, screamed, but suddenly he was actually dreaming, unconscious and completely unaware.

When he awoke, he felt strange, like something was missing. He opened his eyes, scanning the room. He didn't know where he was.

It was a nice house, old and expensive. He tried to use his powers to get a sense of the place: how many people were here, how big the house was, where he was. But nothing happened. He felt nothing.

He was tied to a chair, hands bound too tight behind his back. It was an old chair, heavy and made of thick wood. And he wasn't alone.

In the corner of the room stood a young, white-skinned, dark-haired woman whose eyes were pure black. She was very focused on him, not taking her cold, dark eyes off of him for even a second.

"Where am I?" he said, his voice raspy, his throat dry. Her ominous demeanor made him nervous, but he worked to remain levelheaded.

"You're in Willow Manor," an airy female voice whispered behind him.

He turned his head sharply to see another figure in the room. She wasn't nearly as scary looking as the woman in the corner who was still staring at him. She had beautiful dark skin and short curly dark hair. She even had a smile across her face that seemed inviting and reassuring.

She walked over to his side, looking almost like she was floating to him. Her eyes were so kind; they gave Duncan a false sense of hope.

"I see you've met Jazel," she said, looking at her demonic friend in the corner. "We've been allies for as long as I can remember. She's the strongest Natural I know. But, do you know what's funny?" She turned to look at Duncan, although he could tell nothing she was going to say was a joke. "She can't seem to locate your little friend. Oh, what's her name… Sara."

The kindness on her face was gone, although her ghost-like quality still remained.

"That girl killed one of the most astute members of this family," she said with almost a hiss. "It's her job to pay for what she has done. But we just can't seem to find her. And do you know why?"

Duncan did know. And she knew he knew. It was the same reason his three friends could walk in the sun. He had created a potion for each of them, one that they had to take every day and only worked on the specific person it was created for.

Although most Naturals didn't like vampires, it just so happened that during Duncan's mother's life, she had fallen in love with a vampire. This was why although he didn't know a lot of spells, he knew how to create one that allows vampires to walk in the sun.

At first, the potion had one quality sewn into it: the vampires could walk in the sun. But, after being tracked a few times by other Naturals, he added another quality; they were cloaked. That meant they could not be tracked. All of this was found in his one and only spell book that was given to him by his deceased mother.

It almost made him laugh a little, tied to that chair; his friends were more protected than he was. He had a potion for each of them to walk in the sun and remain stealthy, but he never created anything for himself, nothing to keep him out of the range of spells.

So there he sat, the only one of the group who could be tracked. And, at the moment, the only one who was in danger.

"Ah, yes, a spell," she said, not really impressed. She had moved to stand in front of him.

"Why can't I use my powers?" he asked, looking at the unnamed vampire.

"That would be Jazel," she said, a devious smile crossing her face. "And now that she has complete control over you, you're going to do something for us."

It was at that part of Duncan's story that he stopped. He couldn't remember anything else. Whatever he did for them, he couldn't remember. And he didn't know why they let him go or how he escaped.

***

Astrid and Marcello glanced at each other. They didn't want to say it, but they knew Jazel and they knew the vampire Duncan was talking about. Her name was Mura. Astrid and Marcello had wiped out her evil family a few times, but Jazel and Mura always managed to escape. They decided to keep this to themselves.

"Then how did you three know he was kidnapped if they couldn't find you in the first place?" Astrid said, worried about the missing parts in Duncan's story. However, those questions were not yet going to be answered.

It was at that moment Astrid felt a sharp, painful object puncture straight through her chest. Shock flashed across her face, although irritation and frustration filled her mind. She'd let her guard down.

Astrid hit her knees, and in an instant, Marcello was by her side. The object was still lodged in her chest, though the recently awoken female vampire was standing and making her way across the room.

Suddenly, the female vampire changed forms. From the description in Duncan's story, it appeared to everyone this was the powerful Natural, Jazel, although only Marcello and Astrid actually knew that just meant she was a Natural.

What happened next occurred quickly. The wound in Astrid's chest was fatal to most, but not to a vampire hunter like herself. However, it was a debilitating injury, even for her. In a few moments, against her control, her body was going to shut down. It was a defense mechanism for nearly fatal injuries. Her body would go into a type of hibernation state so it could quickly and efficiently heal the wound. Unfortunately, Astrid didn't have time to sleep. She had to act fast.

Naturals could be killed, but it was tricky. And if it wasn't done right, they only temporarily died. And considering this Natural had the power to shape-shift, she was definitely a serious opponent.

Luckily, Jazel was walking away from Astrid and Marcello. She seemingly no longer considered her a threat since she had delivered such a fatal blow. It was to Astrid's advantage that the Natural didn't know she was a hunter. But she still needed to be quick. To kill a Natural, their heart must be stabbed, their head removed, and, as soon as possible, they needed to be burned.

Astrid looked at Marcello, Jazel having only moved a few feet in front of them. Duncan, Carter, and Grayson surrounded Sara, ready to defend her with their lives. Duncan's eyes began to change color as he began a spell. Astrid gave Marcello a nod, and he ripped the dagger from her body.

She muffled her pain as he took the dagger in his hand, and immediately stabbed the unaware Natural straight into her heart. But they weren't in the clear yet.

Marcello, who, in a split second, had grabbed a large cutting knife from the kitchen and returned a few feet behind Astrid, threw the knife to her.

At the same moment Astrid caught the knife, Jazel began to react to the object impaled through her heart. But Astrid didn't even give her time to turn around. She lifted the large knife, aimed quickly at the Natural's bare neck, and swung.

Suddenly, in the midst of her attack, the uncontrollable sleep began to take hold. She faltered, her strength diminished, but she used all she had left to strike the Natural as hard as she could.

The knife sliced halfway through Jazel's neck. It wasn't enough to kill her, but it was enough to send her vanishing away in fear. Even she, a powerful Natural, would need time to recover from those attacks. Astrid knew she would be back, but for the time being, everyone was safe.

She stood for another moment as the room began to spin around her, Marcello by her side. Suddenly, the darkness took hold. But as she fell to the ground, before Marcello reached to grab her, another set of arms cradled her. It was Carter. He held her in his arms like a child and looked at the gaping wound in her chest. He looked over frantically at Marcello, who had a kind, approving smile across his face.

"What do we do?" Carter said, his voice stuttering with concern. "Is she going to be okay?" Grayson and Sara examined the room and waited to see if Jazel was going to return. Duncan, however, looked sick. He sat on the ground while covering his eyes, letting out random moans to signify he was in some kind of pain.

"She should be fine," Marcello said as he noticed Duncan looking distressed on the floor. "This has happened before. She should wake up in a few hours, and her wound will be healed.

Jazel will be back, though. She hasn't been killed yet. But she is very wounded, and it will take time for her to recover."

He left Astrid with Carter, who still looked at her, concerned, and kneeled next to Duncan on the floor. "Are you all right?" he said gently, placing his hand on Duncan's shoulder.

Duncan took a few deep breaths, lifted up his head, and looked around the room. His face seemed much calmer, no longer contorted with pain. His eyes started to open wider, and he looked at everyone's faces in the room.

"I remembered what happened," Duncan said.

Chapter 10

It took a couple hours for Astrid to awaken. The wound was very severe, even by her standards. It took her body a while to heal. But when she woke up, she was full of life, her injury completely healed. The sun would be up soon.

The whole time she had slept, Carter had kept an eye on her. He sat on the edge of the couch, checking her puncture every few minutes to see how it was healing.

When she began to take breaths and he could hear her heart beating strongly, he moved away from her side, perching himself in the corner of the room, still watching the life return to her body. Although Astrid may have not seen Carter watching over her, Marcello did.

That would be a story for him to tell another day. Right then, there were more important things to talk about.

Before Astrid had passed out, she managed to nearly kill Jazel. Because the Natural was so close to death, her powers temporarily waned. When that happened, the spells she had over Duncan diminished, the cloud covering his memory disappeared, and the control she had over him was gone.

It turned out that when he was kidnapped, Jazel had placed a few strong spells over him. The first rendered him powerless. His strength and energy were still within him, but he couldn't access them. That's why he couldn't tell how many people were in the house or get his bearings on his location.

That caused him the most distress when he first woke up from being unconscious. However, after seeing the ominous woman staring at him in the corner, he had deduced that she may be controlling him somehow.

Before Duncan was able to continue his story, explaining the most important parts, Astrid, who had been listening from the couch, stopped him. "I need to tell you something," she said, determined. "It's been driving me crazy."

Duncan paused and gave her a confused look but allowed her to make her statement.

"You are not a witch," she said very seriously.

"Of course not," Duncan laughed. "I never said I was. I'm a wizard."

"Ugh!" Astrid exclaimed as she grasped her heart, simulating she was in pain. "No, you're not. You're a Natural."

"Jazel was a Natural," Duncan said defensively. "The other woman who spoke to me told me that. I'm not like Jazel."

"No," Astrid demanded. "You're not like Jazel. But you are a Natural. Just like bad vampires aren't like good vampires, they're both vampires, both the same species, but they have different morals. You, however, are technically a Natural. You're the first spell caster I've ever heard use the words witch or wizard in a thousand years. Did you never have a parent or mentor teach you magic?"

Duncan looked at his feet, trying to hide the emotion on his face. Although he'd never had a mentor, he knew his mother should've been his teacher. He stayed silent for a moment and tried to decide if he wanted to tell her or not.

"My mother should've been my teacher," he finally said. "I was too good at hiding my secret from her while she was alive. And only a few days before she was killed, she found out. But a lot was going on in those few days, so there wasn't much time to teach me," he said, looking up at Astrid's eyes. "She gave me one journal of hers just before… she died. It had some personal potions and spells that she had created in there. That's where I found the day-walking potion. She had created it. She told she had been in love with a vampire and created it for him."

Astrid considered that. She and Duncan hadn't gotten off on the right foot, and she wasn't exactly interested in mending that bridge or showing him too much compassion. So, she decided on saying: "Well, we'll find you a mentor soon. But make sure you never use the word witch or wizard again. They may not take you seriously."

"We'll see," he whispered, secretly grateful for her suggestions. He continued his story.

The second spell Jazel had placed on Duncan was a memory loss spell. She didn't cast it until the middle of his conversation with the other woman at the place he was kidnapped. But it was helpful that he finally remembered the rest of the conversation.

He told them that the other woman in the room, who was a vampire, was named Mura. After he said her name, Carter gave Astrid a look to see how she was reacting, and by the shock on her face, she also knew who Mura was.

"Uh-oh," she said as she widened her eyes and looked over at Marcello. "They changed their name."

Duncan decided to ignore her comment for the time being and finish his story. He explained that he was forced by Jazel to tell Mura all about Sara and where she lived; he had no choice in the matter because he had been completely under Jazel's control. That was when a messenger vampire was sent to tell Grayson, Carter, and Sara they had a day to decide whose life was more important: Sara's or Duncan's.

In Mura's mind, Sara had killed someone from her family, so a life had to be taken to replace the one that was lost.

Duncan finished his story by explaining what he thought was the most important information he gained after his memory was returned: he knew where the house was.

When the first group of vampires had come to Carter and Grayson's house, they brought Duncan with them, ready to kill him or Sara when the time was right. However, they didn't anticipate Astrid being there. So, indecently, neither Sara nor Duncan died, just more vampires from Mura's family. Then, a few minutes after the other vampires were killed, Duncan regained his consciousness and control and found himself standing on the doorsteps of his house.

But he finally remembered the steps he took to get there.

Astrid sat still for a moment and waited to see if Duncan was done with his story. She had been waiting anxiously since he revealed the vampire's name was Mura. She was ready for it to be her turn to talk. Duncan almost rolled his eyes as he looked over at her, giving her permission to speak.

"Well, I'm glad all the loose ends are tied up," she said as she patted her hands on her lap and stood, ready to leave. "But, some more important things need to be handled, and I don't think you guys should be a part of it."

"What?" Carter asked with a laugh.

"Marcello and I need to handle this," Astrid said with a serious face. "This situation is more dangerous than you think. Duncan, we need you to tell us how to get to the house."

"No," he said plainly, as if he had anticipated her response and was not shocked. She gave him a grim locked and scowled, ready to open her mouth and speak again, but Duncan beat her to it. "No. Good try, but no. You might be strong, but I can almost guarantee you'll need everyone's help, especially mine. The house is big, and there are a lot of vampires in there. You need a... Natural to help you."

Astrid and Marcello didn't like that plan. They weren't used to working with other people, and those supernatural were basically children. They had no idea what they were up against. So Astrid gave them a little background on Mura.

"It's true," she said as she stood up and began to pace around the room. "Mura is a vampire. But she's not the kind you think she is. Mura is a rare type of vampire. Honestly, Duncan should be honored she even showed herself to him. This type of vampire truly hides in the shadows, even at night. In some ways, they're as tricky to catch as the wind. Marcello and I have never even killed one. We've seen a few, and know of almost all there are, but we've never been able to kill one. Mura is a type of vampire called an Energy.

"There are blood vampires, such as yourselves and Marcello, and there are Energies. Energies don't feed on blood; they feed on strength. They're called Energies because that's what they consume: energy. They suck out your life, strength, hopes, and dreams.

"An Energy cannot be created by another vampire. They're a creation of Naturals to protect themselves from blood vampires. But eventually, their loyalty to their creator drifts away, and they either kill the Natural that created them or just leave.

"They're rarely created anymore, and there is only a handful in the world. But most of them are old and dangerous.

Mura is at least fifteen hundred years old, and I'm sure her family is quite large.

The catch is, Energies can create blood vampires. And Mura is a very old and very powerful leader of what used to be called the West family. But apparently, they changed their name and are now the Willow family."

She stopped pacing and gave her new friends a sincere look of concern as she said, "We don't want your help, but it's not because you're not strong enough to fight. By this point, now that I've killed so many members of her family, she's probably forgotten about what Sara did and is solely focused on killing me."

Astrid sighed and covered her eyes. She wanted to tell them about her curse. Maybe it would make it easier if they knew she was going to die anyway. But she decided to keep that secret to herself a little bit longer.

"What I'm trying to say is, you guys are off the hook," she said with a smile. "Let Marcello and I go risk our lives. We're pros at near-death experiences, and we always win."

Even if it means I die, Astrid thought to herself.

This time, Carter spoke for the group. He stood up, walked over to where Astrid was standing, and smiled as he placed his hand on her shoulder. Astrid stood, wide-eyed.

"In the past forty-eight hours," he began, "you've been attacked, stabbed, basically died, killed at least a couple dozen vampires, and saved the lives of four people you barely know, all while risking your life and the life of your friend. And now you're on the hit list of an apparently almost unstoppable vampire all because of us. Not only do we owe it to you to help, but we want to. So, as Duncan put it earlier, no. Good try, but no. We're going to help, whether you like it or not," he said, giving a flirtatious wink to her at the end of his speech.

Marcello was beginning to feel very sleepy, and he knew why. He looked out the window to see the hint of sunlight peeking over the horizon. He looked at Astrid. "Good, then it's settled," he said. "However, I'm not gifted with your day-walking attributes, and the sun is about to come up. I have to go sleep and get out of the light."

"Let's meet at your house when the sun goes down," Astrid suggested. "We can discuss our plan of action then. I think we could all probably use some sleep, especially if we're going to be alert tonight."

They all agreed to the plan. Marcello drifted home and up his stairs, losing consciousness with every step. He fell asleep as soon as he rested his head on his pillow. However, his last thoughts were strange ones; he considered the feeling to be the same as it must have felt to have an Energy vampire drain your life—although, he would wake up at nightfall. People would never wake up after being drained by an Energy.

Astrid looked at Carter. "I may come by a little earlier than sunset so we can get a head start on making a plan," she said.

"I think that's a great idea," Carter whispered.

Suddenly, Sara decided she needed to make a point. "I don't think what I did was a crime," she said, looking desperately around the room to see how people reacted. "I wish I hadn't killed him," she said, pausing, "but he had no right to turn me."

Grayson put a loving hand on Sara's arm, agreeing with her that the vampire she killed was in the wrong. Astrid yawned a little. She knew how Sara felt, but she also knew the mindset of vampires that lived in families. They didn't think like other vampires. They were very possessive and controlling. If they wanted something, they took it. And they didn't consider anyone else's feelings except that of their family. Ironically, Sara, Grayson, and Carter were at the beginning stages of being a vampire family.

However, Astrid didn't feel like explaining to Sara that the family would never see her changing through her eyes. As soon as Sara turned, she was part of the Willow family, whether she wanted to be or not. Her killing of the vampire who turned her would always be a murder of one family member by another in the eyes of the Willows.

Instead, Astrid agreed but made a point to say vampire families were complicated, although that wasn't the time to discuss it.

"Till dusk, then," Carter said, reminding Astrid of a prince with his sweet eyes, his smell filling her lungs and washing away bad thoughts from her mind.

"Till dusk," she whispered, turning away as she began to blush, waving goodbye as her new friends headed to their home.

However, the plan created by Duncan, Sara, Grayson, and Carter while Astrid and Marcello slept did not include meeting with them at dusk.

Chapter 11

Astrid woke up a little after noon. She brewed a pot of coffee and scavenged for food in her kitchen until she had eaten enough.

She sat at the kitchen table, sipping her coffee while she pondered different ways to handle the vengeful vampire situation. She was still tired.

She was rested just enough to start her day again, but she hadn't slept well. She kept having nightmares involving Mura and the rest of her family.

They didn't involve Astrid, but instead, the dreams featured her new friends. She was worried they wouldn't survive their visit to Willow Manor later that evening. Astrid wasn't scared of death because she knew she would be back. But she feared for the young vampires and the Natural, even if he didn't particularly like her.

Astrid sat at her kitchen table through half a pot of coffee while she considered good and bad ideas for getting rid of the Willow family. Eventually, the clock struck three p.m. She began getting ready to head over to Carter's house to meet everyone. She had thought of a few *good* ideas, although none of them were foolproof.

She considered some plans that involved the help of her new friends and some that didn't. But either way, there were always holes. There were too many unknowns: how big was the family? Were they day-walkers as well? How well-guarded was their house? Astrid could take on a lot of vampires, but she did have a limit. Ten unrespecting vampires? Sure, but fifty? Not even she could do that. And she also wasn't sure how strong her new companions were. So far, all they had done was get in trouble.

Duncan had not filled them in on any details yet. Astrid wasn't even sure how many question he could answer. Either way, they had to deal with it that night. She didn't think Mura would let her quest for vengeance last for more than a day or two.

After Astrid had dressed and readied herself for the day, she checked on Marcello, who was sleeping soundly. He didn't even budge when she entered the room.

She headed back down the stairs and out her front door. She had a strong sense of fear as she left Marcello alone. She was scared they would return during the day, maybe burn the house down, or simply sneak up on Marcello while he was sleeping and kill him.

But she didn't have time to worry. She needed to get to Carter's house. There was a basement area under the ground that Marcello could get to in a flash if something were to happen.

There wasn't a specific time she was supposed to come over, but she figured around 4:00 p.m. would be fine. Marcello would join them all after dusk. Hopefully, they would have a solid plan by then.

Since her new friends knew her strengths, she didn't waste her time driving over to their house. She bolted, leaving nothing but a small trail of dust behind her.

She was at their house in seconds, not even winded from the run. She went up to the door and knocked a few times.

All she heard was silence.

She felt no movement in the house, heard no whispers, and certainly no one answered the door. She didn't hesitate; she walked right in, worried and suspicious of the silence.

She searched and found no one. The last place she looked was Carter's room. She knew it was his by the smell. She closed her eyes and took a deep breath. The crisp aroma filled her senses. His smell was very overwhelming. However, she needed to focus and opened her eyes. The room was large, colored with dark reds and browns. The bed rested up against the wall by a window, and on the bed rested a small, white piece of paper. In an instant, it was in Astrid's hands, opened and being read.

Her first guess when she saw the note on the bed was that it was a ransom note. Maybe they had been kidnapped while she was sleeping, and this note was their captives' terms for their release. However, Astrid wasn't that lucky.

It wasn't a ransom note. It was a short one from Carter, reading, "Sorry, we thought of a better plan and went on without you. See you when we get back." He signed his name in cursive and even put a small smiley face next to it.

It should have made her laugh. He didn't seem like the smiley-face type of guy. But right at that moment, Astrid was angry. And on top of that, she truly feared for the lives of her new friends. She had to find them, and fast.

So Astrid did what she definitely knew how to do: she hunted.

After leaving a small note for Marcello on the door, she took a deep breath through her nose, smelling the air around her. She could pick up scents like an animal. Sometimes, she really thought of herself as a beast, some creature that brutally hunted but was reborn time and time again like a phoenix rising from its ashes.

She stood by the front door, taking in the many senses around her. The smells inside the house were interfering with her tracking skills. She wandered over to the edge of the woods surrounding the property to see if there were any lingering smells left by the group after they started off on their journey.

She walked around the property a few times, unable to pick up anything specific. That was odd to Astrid. Normally, she could pick up a trail easily. Sure, there were physical markers that could be followed. But the easiest way for Astrid to find someone was by following their smell. Out of all the things, no one ever thought to cover up their smell.

But as she walked around, she picked up nothing.

Suddenly, she heard sticks cracking in the woods a few hundred feet ahead. It was the sound of someone, or something, carelessly walking. She listened for a moment, realizing it was only one person. The smell was more human, although it was definitely not a human.

She heard the mysterious person trip, making a sound of frustration. She knew who it was.

It was Duncan.

She rushed to meet him in the woods, stopping only a few feet from his location. "Look who it is," she said with a stern, frustrated look on her face.

For once, he almost looked happy to see her, though it was a short-lived expression. "Good, it's you. I need your help," he demanded.

It took a second for Astrid to regain her composure. She couldn't decide which emotion was going to win out. She was worried for her friends, but she was angry that they had ventured off without her. She decided to abandon them all and focus on a concerned, serious tone. "Where is everyone?" she asked.

She managed a hint of curiosity in her voice, though thinking about the group leaving without her made her angry again.

"Well, I'm not sure," Duncan admitted with a perplexed tone. Astrid became curious as to what had recently transpired between the friends. "They were here one moment, and then they were gone. Not even a trace of them left. Their footprints have vanished."

That explained why Astrid couldn't find their trail. She was trying to catch Carter's smell in the air, but if all traces of them had vanished, his scent must have gone too. "Can't you use a locator spell to find them?" Astrid asked.

Duncan rolled his eyes. "Don't you remember?" he asked condescendingly. "The potion that keeps them alive in the sun also makes them untraceable through locator spells. We just talked about that this morning."

She brushed his demeaning comment off. She had bigger problems than her and Duncan's not-so-friendly relationship. "Where were you all headed?" Astrid asked in a simple tone.

"To Willow Manor," Duncan replied, ready to defend himself if Astrid said anything bad about their decision to leave without her. "We had a good plan. We figured sneaking up on them during the day would be safer. But when we were almost there, they disappeared. Carter, Sara, and Grayson just vanished out of thin air. I'm guessing they are in the manor." He sat on the ground, resting after his hard run to and from the manor.

"Why did you come back?" Astrid asked, considering she thought he would have continued to the manor and tried to free his friends.

"I came to get you," he said in a defeated tone, wiping sweat off his brow. "I'm not sure what to do. They obviously knew we were coming. We had just gotten to the point where we could see the house, and they vanished. But I don't know why they didn't take me. I figured they could see before we even got there, so I didn't go any further, just ran to get away before they decided what to do with me."

Duncan was almost in a state of panic. He sat calmly on the ground, but Astrid could sense his muscles tightening, and she heard his heartbeat rising. He was worried about his friends and scared because of the lack of control he felt. There was nothing he could have done to save them, but if they didn't find a way to get them back, he would blame himself for their disappearance.

However, Astrid was pretty sure why they didn't take Duncan; he had to lead her to the house. They wanted her there, and they wanted to see her coming. Or so she thought.

She decided to explain things as well as she could to Duncan and try to keep him level-headed throughout the evening. It was going to be a long night, and the sun hadn't even gone down yet.

"Jazel probably put up some kind of sensor spell around the grounds of the manor," Astrid began. "That's how they knew you were there. And considering how strong Jazel is, I'm sure most, if not all, of the vampires in the house are day-walkers. Or they may have wolves watching the house during the day time."

Duncan gave Astrid a confused look and thought for a second before he asked her his question. "What kind of wolves?" he wondered.

"Werewolves," Astrid said plainly. "Some families will pay wolves, or even humans sometimes, to watch their homes while they sleep. It's sort of a truce that helps both sides; werewolves watch the vampires, and, in return, the vampires keep an eye on the wolves at night. I haven't heard of any packs around here, but they're good at hiding, so there could be a few in these woods."

He shook his head a little. "We've only had bad experiences with werewolves," he admitted wearily.

"They're not all bad," Astrid said with a reassuring smile, although Duncan did not reciprocate the kindness.

Astrid ushered Duncan into the house. They needed to come up with a better plan since they'd lost three of their group members. The circumstances had changed, and they needed more than a plan of attack on the Willow family. It had become a hostage situation. And they needed to be careful to save their friends.

***

Astrid looked outside. The sun was still up but would probably set in an hour or so. Marcello would be waking soon. Astrid stood up, excited. "This is a great plan," she said, smiling while looking at Duncan. He had a much calmer mood about him and even shared a quick smile with her. "It's almost foolproof. With your magic, my speed and strength, and a little luck, we can accomplish everything we need before midnight!"

Duncan was happy too. The plan really was a good one. Although the people they were up against were strong, their plan was probably too clever for them. They were ready to fight, and they were ready to win.

Astrid packed up her things, which had been sprawled out on the floor by the fireplace as she and Duncan planned their rescue mission. But as Astrid stood up, stakes in hand, she had a strange sensation wash over her. Duncan could feel the mysterious energy radiating from Astrid. It was definitely some kind of magic, and it felt dark. He gave her a concerned look.

"I think something's wrong," she whispered, a bit of fear in her eyes.

And before anyone could say another word, Astrid screamed.

Chapter 12

Carter, Grayson, and Sara opened their eyes, lost. They looked at each other, each expressing similar emotions of confusion and fear. The capture wasn't supposed to happen, and they could have never planned for it either.

They stood in a small room filled with eight other vampires looking at them hungrily and with stakes in their hands. Whether they were supposed to or not, those vampires wanted to kill Carter, Grayson, and Sara. And it clearly wouldn't be a pleasant death.

Sara took a step back, concerned. She stood behind Grayson, holding tight to his arm. They were all scared.

Everyone's attention turned as the door in the room opened, and a beautiful, dark-skinned, female vampire entered the room. She almost floated as she walked. Her face was calm and inviting. She looked kind.

Carter was the first to catch on. He remembered the description of the vampire from Duncan's story: beautiful, dark skin, curly dark hair, kind eyes. *This must be her*, he thought—*Mura*.

"We didn't expect you so soon," she said, her voice soft and pleasant but suspiciously so. "Most vampires prefer to attack at night."

"You must be Mura," Carter said bravely from the other side of the room. The hungry vampires gave a deep growl as if he had issued some kind of insult. He started to think quickly, making a new plan. "We didn't come to attack you. We came to talk."

What Carter didn't realize was that family vampires didn't do a lot of talking with other vampires. They preferred actions as their means of communication with vampires outside of their family. However, his stoic tone and fearless posture intrigued Mura, so she decided to play along.

"Oh, really," she said, not acting surprised. "You didn't come to kill us? That seems to have been your plan every other time you've encountered my family."

What Carter also didn't know was there was no way to argue or talk with vampire families. They had gone past the point of reason when it came to their flesh and blood. If they thought someone had done them wrong, there was nothing they could do to get out of it. But Carter continued anyway.

"Yes, we wanted to talk," he continued. "This whole situation is a big misunderstanding. We came to set things right."

Mura gave a sweet smile, but it wasn't a pleasant one. It was the type of smile someone gives after they have finished insulting you.

"Well, aren't you precious," she said, ignoring Carter and looking directly at Sara. "You seem scared, hiding behind your friend. Is he your lover?"

Carter rolled his eyes a bit, which was the worst thing he could have done. He just gave more fuel to Mura. "Oh," she said, surprised. "I'm guessing she used to be yours, then... Carter, is it?"

No one was amused. Sara stood, looking down and blushing. Carter and Grayson were irritated with past feelings being brought to the surface against their will.

"Do you mind if we just talk about the issues at hand?" Carter asked as pleasantly as he could be considering his current emotional state.

Mura was amused. She decided to let Carter talk, just for the sake of wasting time. "Okay, then," Mura said. "Why don't you tell me your side of the story? But be quick. I'm running out of patience for the day. And I have a surprise I can't wait for you all to see."

Carter looked at his friends. They were all very worried. Whatever the surprise was, it couldn't be good. But Carter decided to go for it. He put his best charming face on and explained, in the most entertaining way he could, their side of the story.

He described how Sara was attacked and never wanted to be a vampire. He said that her reaction when she first changed was normal, and it wasn't her fault that her rage took control.

He then tried to explain how the first group of vampires to attack the house was a surprise, and that Astrid didn't know the situation when she walked in the door. She was simply defending herself and her new friends who were injured in their own home.

Finally, he talked about the attack at Astrid's house and how that was a similar mistake. Astrid had still not been filled in on the situation, so she reacted in defense. She was just trying to protect her friends and her house.

Mura sat quietly and patiently as Carter tried to make his case. But to her, it was like watching a movie. She was entertained by the story, but at the end of the day, it didn't matter. Their bad deeds had been done, and there was nothing they could say to talk themselves out of the pain she was going to put them through.

"What a good story," she said, looking more suspicious every time she talked. "May I show you your surprise now?"

Grayson took the stage. "What about the information you just received?" he asked aggressively. "Don't you want to talk about what he just told you?"

Mura looked at Grayson, her eyes cold and uncaring, though she still had a smile on her face. "No," she said directly. "I don't care. And I'd really like to show you your surprise."

"What if we don't want to see it?" Sara said, her voice shaking.

"Why, my dear," Mura began, "you don't have a choice. My children will lead you down the hall for tonight's entertainment."

The hungry and vicious-looking vampires that surrounded the friends began to lunge at them, encouraging them to move and make their way out the door. Sara was the most frightened. That wasn't the life she was meant to live. Even as a vampire, she felt helpless, fearful, and weak.

The group of three had been separated when they began making their way out of the door. All three of them were spread out amongst the vicious vampires threatening to attack at any minute. They all paced down the hall like a herd, following Mura to wherever her surprise was hidden.

Carter was the calmest. He kept a stoic face, not letting the wild, snarling vampires cause him any visible fear. Grayson was worried mostly about Sara, who was the furthest in the back, looking more and more scared by the minute.

After walking down the long, dark hallway, they made their way into a room much larger than the rest. The whole room as white; every chair and wall, and even the ground was white painted wood. A large white curtain hung from the ceiling, covering up what Carter could only guess was their surprise.

The three vampires were led to one side of the room, and the wild eight made their way out of the door, closing it behind them.

An old "friend" of theirs appeared near the window on the far side of the room. Her neck was almost healed, but undoubtable anger raged in her eyes. A devious smile crept across Jazel's face. She was glad they were all finally there.

Carter tried to take a step forward, attempting to make another statement about it all being an accident. Before he could get a word out, he stumbled into an invisible wall that threw him back and to the floor.

Carter hit the floor, his friends quickly by his side. They all looked up, examining the area he had struck. There was nothing there. Confused, he stood up slowly, reaching his hand toward the same area. Unexpectedly, he touched some invisible barrier that had been placed between them and the surprise hidden under a large cloth.

"That would be Jazel's doing," Mura said, looking approvingly at Jazel. "We want to make sure you don't leave before the show is over. You have a little bit of wiggle room, but the energy field completely surrounds you." Mura walked over to a cord hanging behind the hidden object in the room. The curtain made a circle around the object, making it impossible to tell what was inside.

However, before the curtain was lifted and the surprise was revealed, Sara was the first to notice the smell in the room. "I smell human blood," she said, looking for confirmation from her friends.

But Mura took the stage before Carter or Grayson could answer. "It's time for the main attraction," Mura said as she pulled the cord, allowing the curtain to fall directly to the ground. Sara gasped and covered her mouth, tears beginning to rise in her eyes. "I told you it would be a surprise."

In front of them was a young human girl, and one that they all knew very well. Two years ago, when Sara became involved with the supernatural world, she had confided in a friend of hers about what was happening.

Unfortunately, she decided to stay away from Sara and supernatural friends. She had tried to persuade Sara to leave Carter, Grayson, and Duncan. She said the humans and the supernatural beings were better off staying away from each other.

But Sara didn't want to stay away. She had fallen in love with Grayson. But now, as she stood fearful, staring at her friend and looking at the situation she was in, she did have regret. If she had just stayed away, none of this would have happened. She wouldn't be a vampire and she wouldn't be in this horrible situation.

All contact had been cut off between this one friend and the group. She didn't want any part of the danger, and they respected her wishes. But there she was. Iron cuffs held her wrists and ankles to an iron chair placed in the middle of the room. Her head was down, and she wasn't moving.

"What have you done to her?" Sara demanded.

"Oh, she's fine," Mura said, rubbing her hand across the sleeping girl's back. "For now."

Grayson's chest was rising and falling rapidly, his breathing audible in the mostly silent room. Carter clenched and unclenched his hands over and over, the rage filling him to the point of snapping. He began screaming at Mura, with

Grayson chiming in as well, both of them saying anything they could think of to get her to let the innocent human go. But Mura didn't care that the girl was innocent or that she didn't want to be a part of the supernatural world. Mura only cared about revenge.

"Jazel, would you be so kind as to wake up our new friend?" Mura asked her ominous Natural cohort. "I'd like everyone to be awake for this next part of the show."

Within a second, a soft moan crept out of the girl's lips. She began to raise her head, her eyes slowly beginning to acknowledge the room. She tried to move her hands, her legs. She began to wake up much faster as the adrenaline started to pump through her body. She was scared, confused.

"Wake up, my dear. Your friends are here," Mura said with a smile.

"Mel!" Sara shouted from her small corner. "Mel, it's okay. We're here."

She opened her eyes wide and saw her old friends standing in front of her.

"Sara?" she whispered, her voice hoarse and raspy. "What's going on?" She still struggled to release her hands and feet from their chains.

"I think I'll answer that," Mura began. "And you, my dear, are the main attraction."

Mel looked frightened. Her friends in the room gave her no comfort. Sweat began to build up on her forehead. She couldn't speak. Her breathing became labored. Sara noticed the small mat of blood on the right side of Mel's head. That must have been the blood she smelled before the curtain went down.

"What are you going to do to her?" Grayson demanded, his hands pushing on the invisible barrier keeping them trapped.

"I guess I can tell you if you really want to know."

Mura picked up a long, thick, metal dagger that rested on one of the windowsills and began to walk over again to Mel. "I'm going to do something fun. You see, I decided I wasn't ready to kill you three yet. I wanted to make you suffer a little before I did the final deed of killing you. But I had a problem. Do you know what that is?"

Everyone looked at Mura, terrified for their friend. They were tired of her games.

"Well, I'll tell you," she continued. "The hunter is my problem."

Everyone but Mel knew what she was talking about: Astrid.

"Every time I try to attack," she said, almost gritting her teeth a bit, "this vampire hunter girl ruins my plans. She's too quick, smart, and strong. My family members are no match for her strengths. So, I need to get rid of her."

"Then why do you need Mel?" Grayson interjected. "Just let her go!"

"But here's the fun part," Mura said, her face lighting up with revenge. "I need your friend to kill the hunter. And I need your friend to make you suffer. I want you to watch as she slowly and painfully dies, all the while realizing your hunter friend is dying as well."

Sara was speechless. She was helpless. Her friend was going to die, and it was going to be all her fault. Tears began to fill her eyes as she touched the barrier gently, looking at her friend.

Suddenly, something changed in Sara. She looked out the clear barrier straight at Mura and let out a low growl. Carter and Grayson didn't even notice the change, but Sara looked like a monster.

Mel was petrified, and she had a good right to be. There was nothing Sara or her friends could do to save her. She only hoped Astrid or Duncan would be there soon. Maybe they could save Mel.

"But you don't even know where the hunter is," Carter said, making sure to leave out Astrid's name in case Mura didn't know what it was yet.

"It doesn't matter where she is," Mura said, uninterested in what the other vampires in the room had to say. She was ready to start her show. "Jazel has made it so Mel and the hunter are… connected. Meaning whatever I do to Mel will also happen to the hunter."

"But she's stronger than a human," Carter said, terrified for Astrid, wishing he could escape the barrier to find her and protect her.

"True," Mura admitted. "But Jazel has also taken care of that. For the time being, your friend's curse is gone, and she's nothing more than a useless, vulnerable human."

"Curse?" Carter said to himself, although everyone was equally confused.

"Oh, that's interesting," Mura said, intrigued. "She didn't tell you about her hunter curse? Well, I'll save that surprise for later. I'll let her little vampire companion tell you after I've killed her."

The talking was over. Mura gave a quizzical look to Jazel, as if to ask if everything was ready. Jazel gave a slow nod, and with one swift motion, Mura jabbed the dagger into Mel's left shoulder. It was the first, but not the last, strike.

Chapter 13

Mel screamed and convulsed in her chair. She couldn't bear the pain. Sara, Carter, and Grayson looked on in horror; Carter frequently cursed Jazel and Mura, slamming his hands on the barrier in a desperate attempt to free himself. Although he was sad for Mel, all he could think about was Astrid. If what Mura said was true, Astrid was feeling everything Mel felt. And she was going to die when it was all over.

Mura removed the dagger from Mel's shoulder then lifted it again and plunged the blade into her left thigh. Mel screamed and convulsed, tears streaming down her face.

"I also forgot to tell you the best part," Mura said, pausing what was sure to be a long torture session. "Jazel has made it so that even when the blood loss and injuries would be bad enough to kill a human, they won't die until I feel like stopping. Jazel will keep them alive until I feel like they have felt enough pain, and then they will die."

"Please," Carter begged. "She didn't know. She was just protecting us."

"Oh, she knows," Mura said as she ripped the dagger out of Mel's thigh. "She has killed my family more than once. Now it is time for her to pay."

***

Astrid screamed, reaching her right hand over to her left shoulder. "Fuck!" she shouted, confused. Astrid leaned forward as if she was going to fall, but Duncan jumped toward her and embraced her as best he could.

"What's wrong?" he asked with wide eyes filled with confusion. He had his hand on her upper back and a wet substance began trickling down his fingers. Astrid looked to Duncan, her eyes truly full of fear. This was the first time he saw fear in Astrid's eyes. He wanted to help her, to comfort her. She was strong, and for her to be worried made him very worried. He longed for the darkness of night so Marcello could be by her side.

She looked at her shoulder, blood rushing down her back. The pain was more intense than normal. After a few seconds, she realized the wound wasn't starting to heal. Suddenly, another pain ruptured through her left thigh. She fell to her right knee, hands shaking from fear and pain. Blood streamed from her wounds. She could see her muscle and bone.

She stared at Duncan. "I'm not healing," she said, gritting her teeth through the pain, trying to hide her fear. "Some days," she struggled to say, "I have wished that I would not heal." Duncan looked at her with confusion and sadness. "But today, I would like to live. We… have to think of something," she forced out as she groaned from pain of not healing.

He was next to her on the floor, his hand still on her back. He wanted to help her, to comfort her. But he didn't know what to do.

She screamed again, and this time, a wound appeared on her upper right arm. It looked as if a knife had gone directly through her.

Astrid doubled over and gasped in air, unable to scream, cry, or breathe. A new slash appeared straight through her stomach.

She was suffering. Her left shin took the brunt of the next blow, and Astrid fell to the floor, lying on her back. She took quick, sharp breaths, screaming every time she endured another injury.

"I'm not healing," she forced out again, her voice shaky, weak. Her whole body shook all over. Another attack shot straight through her right thigh. She screamed, arching her back in agony. Astrid had felt pain before, but nothing like that. She had no time to prepare for the pain.

The wounds kept coming, in her shoulder, her arms, her legs, down her back, through her stomach. The blood spilled all over the hardwood floor. Rivers of blood came out of every direction from her body. Pools of blood filled the floor around her. Her bone and muscle was exposed in many spots.

Duncan sat on his knees, tightly holding her hand. She squeezed his hand with all her might, but he never let go. He wondered why his hand didn't break. She was so strong. But then, he began to realize what she had been saying a few moments before. She wasn't healing, and her strength was gone: she was human.

Whatever was happening to her, she wasn't going to recover from it unless he did something. He thought for a moment, finding it hard to focus through her screams. He wanted to hold her, to make the pain go away. He'd never seen someone suffer so much. All he wanted to do was help her. But in his panic, he couldn't think of how.

Finally, he thought of a spell. He grasped her hand tight, looking at her eyes. They were beginning to bruise from how tight she was holding them shut, small tears slipping out from the corners. But she was in too much pain to cry.

"Astrid," he said through her cries, "you have to look at me. I can make the pain go away."

She thrashed her head back and forth, the injuries still appearing all over her body.

He grabbed her face. "You have to look at me. Open your eyes, God damn it!"

She looked up at him, her eyes weak and blood red. Her breath was shallow. Tears began escaping her now-open eyes. She fought to keep them open, screaming at every sudden pain. Duncan began whispering unknown words to himself, his eyes white with energy. A sudden calmness washed over Astrid. The pain began to numb, and her breath slowed and deepened, her eyes still fighting to close.

She stared at him for a while, but she couldn't tell the actual amount of time. He whispered his people's words under his breath, looking into her deeply wounded eyes. He was using two spells: one to heal and one to relieve pain. He had to look into her eyes to use the spell to take away the pain. But if she happened to pass out from exhaustion, the healing spell could be done while she slept.

Once he completed the spells, however, for a brief instant, he would feel all the pain he took away from her. The spell he used would do no harm to him, but to take away the pain, it had to be felt by another.

Finally, after Astrid took in one last deep breath, her eyes closed. Her exhaustion won over. But the pain had subsided anyways. He looked around at her body. The wounds seemed to have stopped appearing. The newer wounds still bled, but the older ones had healed; his spell was working.

He stared at her for a long time, sending as much healing magic as he could to her. His phone rang. He continued to focus on his magic but answered when he saw it was Carter.

"Is Astrid with you? Where are you?" Carter yelled.

"Yes, she's with me. We're at the house," he said, pausing for a moment to continue with his spell. "Where are you?"

"We'll be there soon," Carter said, and he hung up the phone.

Duncan took this as a sign that Astrid was safe. He saw that the wounds had almost all completely healed, and he hoped in a few hours, her own healing abilities would return. So he let go of her hand, discontinued the spell, and felt the most shocking wave of pain rush through his body. His chest jutted forward. He couldn't breathe or scream, his eyes widened, his body feeling every bit of pain he had taken from Astrid.

But then, in an instant, it was gone. Duncan hit the floor, losing all consciousness, having passed out from the pain.

***

After several minutes of relentlessly torturing the innocent human, Mura decided it was enough. She gave Jazel the signal, and instantly, the life disappeared from Mel's eyes as her head rolled back. Blood covered the floor. Unfortunately, Duncan's healing and pain-relieving spells did not work on Mel. She felt every stab of the dagger as it entered her body and as it left.

Sara sat on the floor crying. She was beside herself and inconsolable. Grayson and Carter both stood, resting their hands on the invisible barrier, staring at their dead friend covered in blood. Carter thought of Astrid, wondering if she was okay, all the while aware she probably wasn't.

Suddenly, the energy field was gone. Carter and Grayson had to catch themselves as they fell forward, the wall they were resting on no longer there. The door to the room opened, and the eight wild vampires entered the room again as Jazel exited.

"Now," Mura said, breaking her silence. "I hope you all enjoyed that and learned something. This is not your last surprise. There are definitely a few more to come. But for now, you're free to go."

As she said this, she motioned to the door. The eight vampires pushed and prodded the friends until they began moving out of the door. Carter and Grayson screamed a few more insults at Mura as they left the room. Even Sara, in her sadness, managed a deathly look at Mura as she walked through the door. That experience would prove to make Sara a stronger vampire.

After the eight vampires escorted them outside, the large wooden door they had not entered from closed behind them. They stood for a second, taking in what had just happened. They ran to the edge of the woods where they had first been kidnapped, and Carter found his phone lying on the ground. He picked it up and immediately called Astrid, but she didn't answer. So he called Duncan. Once he found out Astrid was at his house with Duncan, they ran quickly to see if their friend was okay.

***

They made it to the house in a few minutes. They ran fast, but not nearly as quickly as Astrid could. They bolted through the heavy wooden door, all taken aback by the strong, dense smell of blood filling the air. Carter ran in first, only to find Duncan and Astrid unconscious on the ground in front of the fireplace, Astrid lying in a large pool of blood.

Suddenly, Duncan began to stir. Carter rushed over to them, picking up Astrid and holding her in his arms. Fear filled his mind. She couldn't be dead. She was too strong to die.

Duncan groaned and opened his eyes. He saw Carter cradling Astrid in his arms. "You didn't even check first to see if I was okay," Duncan said, giving Carter a little smile.

Grayson and Sara entered the room, making their way over to Duncan.

"Is she okay?" Carter asked anxiously. He gave Duncan a very serious look, ignoring his joking comment.

"I think so," he said, still a bit groggy from passing out. "The craziest thing just happened. Where've y'all been?"

Carter interrupted, still worried about Astrid. "Are you sure she's okay? She doesn't seem to be breathing."

Duncan looked at her and shrugged. "Honestly, man, I don't know. I did everything I could to help her. I healed her wounds. This might just be her hunter self-healing again."

"Unless she's still a human," Grayson said. "Then she might be dead."

Carter looked down at Astrid, staring intently. He wasn't going to give up on her yet. He would hold her all night if he had to. He wasn't ready to lose her yet.

"How do you know she was human?" Duncan asked.

Grayson and Sara explained their scarring story to Duncan while Carter kept an eye on Astrid. Duncan was shocked by what they said, but at least what had happened to Astrid made more sense.

Still, he told his story of his day with Astrid almost dying from unpreventable wounds. And how he healed her and took her pain away. He kept out the part where he had to feel for a moment what she had felt. It gave him chills thinking about that pain.

They sat for a while, happy to be home but worried about what their next surprise from Mura would be and all trying to process the scene of horror from earlier in the day as they watched their friend be tortured to death.

They realized the next time Mura showed herself, they would really need Astrid's help. This made them more anxious when they weren't sure if she was going to wake up or not. But after a short while, everyone calmed down and began to rest.

They stayed in the living room, Carter unwilling to move Astrid to any other position until she woke up. Everyone but Carter drifted to sleep for a few hours, until suddenly, Astrid gasped for breath.

Chapter 14

Astrid clutched her heart tightly, gasping in as much air as she could. She made a sound of pain, pushing and fighting hard to get out of Carter's arms, and turning till she was resting on her hands and knees. She made sounds as if she were having an asthma attack, her hand clutching her chest hard. She felt like she was breathing through glass shards.

She rolled back over onto her back again, everyone in the room wide awake, giving her space. Carter wanted to help, but he wasn't sure what to do. The last time she woke up from almost dying, it wasn't so dramatic.

As she lay on her back, her breath began to slow and deepen. Whatever was preventing her from breathing was slowly passing. Her face calmed, and her hand fell by her side, no longer clutching her chest. Her eyes slowly opened, no longer blood red from before. She blinked a few times, staring straight at the ceiling, then began processing what was around her.

She saw her new friends all staring at her, their faces filled with relief. She managed a soft smile, though in her eyes, they could see she was tired. The sleep she had just been through helped heal her, but it didn't give her rest.

She looked over at Carter, whose arm was very bruised, although the color was quickly turning back to normal. "I'm sorry," she whispered, looking him in the eyes. She had broken his arm when she violently separated herself from him, although it was already almost healed. He just smiled, happy she wasn't dead.

She looked over at Duncan, who sat on the floor in front of the couch; a few blankets lay under him. She stood up, walked over to him, and to everyone's surprise, she gave him a big hug, whispering, "Thank you," in his ear.

After a second to recover from the shock, his body relaxed and he returned the hug, glad Astrid was alive. Having gone through that terrible event, he felt a little closer to her. In only a few days, Astrid had gone from a complete stranger to someone he never though he would trust to a close friend, although there was still a lot to learn about each other.

Astrid looked outside after a long embrace with Duncan. The sun was finally setting on this unusually cool May day. Marcello would be at the house soon. But before she could point that out to everyone in the room, not a second after the sun set, Marcello came bursting through the door, rushing to Astrid, lifting her off the ground, and embracing her tight in his arms.

"I heard you screaming," he said, his eyes closed and his face buried in her shoulder. "I thought you were dead."

Astrid felt bad for her lifelong friend. She knew it must have been agonizing to hear her screaming for so long and then hear the silence that followed, knowing there was nothing he could do but wait till the sun went down to see if she was alive.

He couldn't risk leaving the house with the sun up. He could die within seconds of being out in the light. But something like Astrid's screams could wake him from his deep sleep and render him helpless, waiting for the sun to go down to check on his friend.

Astrid smiled and hugged him tightly back. She was glad he was there.

"I think we all need to talk," Carter said after a few moments. He didn't want to rush Astrid's recovery, but there was a lot at risk, and they needed a plan.

They needed to talk about Mura.

***

After hearing everything that had happened that day, the first thing Astrid did was withdraw from Bella Sleigh College. After missing almost, the whole first week, it didn't look like she would have much time for class in the near future. So she borrowed a computer and withdrew from school, realizing the last few months of her curse cycle would not be spent in relaxation.

Carter looked down when he asked, "why didn't you tell us you knew Mura?"

Astrid looked in shock and sighed, "I just… didn't trust you yet. There is a lot I haven't told you."

"Like your curse?" Carter asked.

"Not now, please" she said as she caught Duncan's eye.

She wasn't in the mood to worry about Mura or her curse. She was tired, exhausted, really. The minutes or so of surprise torture, even with the help from Duncan, had taken a lot out of her. Although she slept for an hour or so, her body did all it could to heal her, but she didn't get any rest. She wanted to sleep, eat, and drink an ocean of water.

She looked at Duncan, who was the only one in the house who had human needs. "Is there any food or water I can have?" she asked almost desperately. "Preferably both."

"Yes," Duncan said, looking a little hungry himself. "Come with me to the kitchen, and we can fix something."

She wondered about the water. Only a few days ago, it was broken. She hoped desperately it was fixed.

To her surprise, it was. Apparently, when Carter had said it acted up a lot, he wasn't lying. *They must have gotten it fixed,* she thought.

Astrid and Duncan made some sandwiches while the vampires sat and watched. It used to be weird for Astrid to spend time with vampires knowing they never ate human food. They either watched or vanished for a bit while people ate. But after a few hundred years, it became normal to Astrid, just another part of life.

However, Duncan didn't look quite as comfortable as she did. Even though he lived with vampires, he wasn't used to their staring or lack of eating. He sat almost nervously through the meal. Astrid tried to loosen the mood by joking about the vampires being creepy for staring. It helped a little since they ended up leaving the room while Astrid and Duncan finished their meal in peace.

After eating, Astrid was once again overcome with the urge to sleep. But she had no idea when Mura would attack again. And she was definitely done playing nice. She was ready to put an end to Mura and she family forever.

Marcello and Astrid decided the best tactic would be to surprise Mura at her home. This time they suggested Duncan transport them all into the house, allowing them the element of surprise. Also, they would all go together, not separated this time. Astrid had a lot of weapons, mainly wooden-bullet guns and stakes. She had an almost endless supply of both in her basement. If they could even manage to injure the vampires in the manor, the wood inside their skin would make them much weaker.

The wooden bullet guns were a new addition to her arsenal. In a normal gun, a plain wooden bullet would shatter and never make it out of the barrel. But she had convinced a Natural back in the 80s to make bullets that were magically strong, but still had the effect of wood. She didn't use them often, but she figured they could come in handy now.

Their biggest worries were Mura and Jazel. Astrid wasn't exactly sure if a wooden stake would kill an energy vampire like Mura because she had never killed one before, and Jazel was strong and tough to kill. Astrid cursed herself for not finishing the job when she had the chance. Jazel probably now had a personal grudge against her, which wasn't a good thing.

A lot of Astrid's plan relied on Duncan. Normally, she and Marcello could handle a situation with surprise attacks and brute force. However, the situation was unique. Not only were they dealing with an Energy vampire, they were dealing with a powerful Natural. They needed magic to help level the playing field.

Unfortunately, Duncan didn't know as much as Astrid was hoping. "Don't you have spell books stored somewhere?" Astrid asked, a little irritated by her inexperienced Natural.

"They were lost when my home was burnt down," he solemnly said.

That's what fire protection spells are for, Astrid thought to herself, wondering how amateur of a Natural his mother must have been. She had never met a Natural who didn't fire-protect their spell books. But she wouldn't say that to Duncan. She wasn't that heartless.

"Then we need to borrow some," she said instead. Spell books were often passed down through generations, but they could also be made or bought from certain locations. However, she couldn't buy them by herself. Duncan would need to go with her, but that would mean they would have to drive. "Do you know any transportation spells?"

"No," he said, also not happy with his short spectrum of knowledge. The few spells he knew were good ones, but they weren't helpful enough.

Astrid sighed a little. The main reason she didn't want to drive was her exhaustion. She wanted to get there quickly, buy the books, and get home early so she could sleep a few hours before dawn. She didn't want a repeat of a few days ago when she attacked the first large group of vampires and then passed out afterwards. And Duncan was a Natural, so he needed about as much sleep as a human, meaning she couldn't make him drive all the way there.

She sighed again, this time a bit more exaggerated. "I guess we need to drive there, then," she said, covering her eyes. "As you guys have seen; I don't do well without sleep."

Marcello gave her a confused look. "Then why don't I drive?" he asked. "I can get you there before sunrise and then run home. Once you've rested, you both can drive home."

She looked at him wide-eyed for a second. She really needed to sleep. That was the most obvious plan, and she didn't even think of it. She nodded her head in agreement. "Okay."

Blessings was near Fort Collins in northern Colorado. The closest spell bookstore that Astrid knew of was in Pueblo, Colorado, about three hours away. That would give Astrid a good few hours, enough to function for a day.

If they left soon, they could get there an hour or so after midnight. Duncan wondered if the store would be open, and Astrid gave him a funny look. "It's a spell bookstore," she said sarcastically. "They never close."

They gathered a few things and snacks for the road and headed on their way. But Carter stopped them before they left.

"I think I should go with you," Carter said, talking only to Astrid as Marcello and Duncan sat waiting in the car, Sara and Grayson listening in the other room. "It's not safe for you all to go so far away."

Astrid laughed. "I think we'll be safer than you guys," she said, appreciating his concern. "'Far away' is the better place to be right now. I'm more worried about leaving you all alone." She smiled at him. She wished he could come. But she needed to rest, not stay up flirting with Carter.

She gave him a soft pat on the shoulder, saying she'd be back soon, and turned to walk toward the car. But she stopped, turned around so quickly the wind blew Carter's hair and she gave him a short, but lovely kiss. He paused, not expecting it, but put his hand gently on her face. But before he could lean more into the kiss, she turned away, scampering down toward the car almost tripping on her own feet. Carter let out a giggle.

Astrid smiled at him as she sat in the car. But the smile faded as she turned and thought about the road ahead. She was worried for her friends they were leaving behind; it really was probably safer to get far away. But they needed to end their problem, which meant they had to fight. And with Jazel on Mura's side, they needed magic to win.

Marcello started the car. Duncan sat in the front, the seat leaned back, while Astrid lay down in the back. The three vampires left behind stood in the doorway as the others left, hoping they would return soon and safely.

Astrid's sleep was restless. It wasn't the moving car or the cramped space—Astrid could sleep almost anywhere. It was the worry. They had a plan, and she knew it could work. Once again, they just needed a little luck on their side.

Unfortunately, last time, they hadn't had any. And she couldn't help but worry about what Mura and her family were capable of and how angry Jazel was at Astrid for almost killing her.

The car finally stopped a little after 1:00 a.m. Astrid and Duncan stretched in their seats, wishing they had more sleep. They were both so tired from the day before. They had been through a lot.

There were no lights on inside, but Astrid knew that would be the case. Duncan looked at the building with curiosity and confusion. It was a real bookstore; one regular people would go to during the day. It was a very small building, about the size of a little millhouse. It stood alone on the side of an old, quiet highway that rarely saw cars. He wondered how it stayed in business.

"It's not the humans who keep this place funded," Marcello said, noticing Duncan's confusion.

"It looks closed," Duncan said, pointing out the obvious.

"Come on, Duncan," Astrid said, giving him an encouraging pat on the back. "You're a Natural. Don't look for the obvious."

He looked at the building for a minute, pondering what Astrid had said. *Maybe it's a cloaking spell*, he thought. And once he did, the magic protecting the building sensed the presence of a Natural and instantly revealed itself to him, illuminating all around.

The building was huge and bright, very modern-looking with sharp edges and neutral colors. He could see all the books inside through the well-lit windows, and people were wandering around inside. His eyes lit up. "That's amazing," he said to himself.

Astrid walked over to the door and knocked. She and Marcello couldn't see the uncloaked store unless they were invited in. Only Duncan could see past the magic.

Before someone answered, Astrid handed Duncan a huge wad of cash. "What is this for?" he said confused.

"You have to pay for these books," Astrid answered, laughing a little. "They aren't free, and they come at a heavy price."

Just then, a woman answered the door. Astrid and Marcello didn't know her. The woman who used to work there was an older Natural named Tina. The Natural at the door was still relatively young. Although in human years she was probably in her late fifties, she looked to be in her late thirties, and she would for many more years. Naturals took a while to age.

When Astrid and Marcello saw the woman, they smiled and greeted her kindly like they would anyone else, and the woman responded pleasantly. Her name was Paige.

Duncan's face was filled with shock. Astrid turned around, ready to introduce the two Naturals to each other and start the spell book searching process, but Duncan spoke before she could.

"Mom...?"

Chapter 15

After a few hours of waiting, Grayson decided to leave the house. It wasn't very safe, but it was late at night, and everyone needed to eat. Unlike Marcello, who kept a stash of blood in a cooler at his house, Grayson had never thought to do that, and neither had Carter.

Instead, he went out into the woods, in the opposite direction of Willow Manor, and hunted for some large prey; he carried three water bottles in a small backpack to drain the animal and bring back the blood to his family.

Although small, Carter, Grayson, and Sara were a family, with Duncan being their adopted member. Grayson had created Carter a hundred or so years ago, making Carter his protégé. Grayson had spent a good deal of his time alone before then, going through phases of being a vicious killer and others where he only fed on animal blood.

What he learned was that animal blood was never enough. It could satisfy a vampire for a long time, even a few months. But, it'd be almost like a slow death. Vampires would get weaker and weaker while consuming only animal blood. Eventually, vampires had to feed on human blood, or they would die.

Maybe it was the curse of being a vampire that made human blood so necessary, or maybe there was some nutrient only humans possessed that vampires needed to survive. Either way, they needed it.

When Carter and Grayson had first moved to town three years ago, Carter was the first to notice Sara. She reminded him of the sun, which he had not seen for at least a hundred years. But he remembered what it looked like, what it felt like, and being around her made him feel like he was walking in the sun again.

After getting to know each other in school, they spent a few months as a couple. It didn't take long for Sara to realize he was different, that he was a vampire. And it didn't take long for her to be put in danger.

An enemy from Carter and Grayson's past had come to find them in Blessings. But instead, he found Sara. To Carter's surprise, every vampire had the same feeling of walking in the sun around her. He didn't know what it was, but something radiated from her, attracting vampires who came near her.

Unfortunately, Carter and Grayson's enemy decided he wanted a taste of Sara's blood. Grayson was the one to save her, giving her his blood to heal her wounds. That act put Grayson in a new light in Sara's eyes, and she struggled to connect with Carter after that day.

Eventually, she chose Grayson, although Carter tried his hardest to get her back. But her love for Grayson had grown too strong, and Carter backed off, longingly looking off in the distance as he watched his creator take the woman he loved.

Recently, the tension had gotten worse, which mainly just irritated Duncan. Sara's recent change had caused her emotions to be less controllable, making it more difficult for her to commit to one man.

Not only that, but Sara was jealous. Her wild emotions caused her to become territorial of both Carter and Grayson, and Carter's attraction to Astrid was not settling well, although she was good at hiding it.

Shortly after he left, Grayson returned with three full bottles, his fangs still out and blood on his face and clothes. "Deer," he said, throwing each of them a bottle. Grayson was by far the best hunter, although Sara was surprisingly good at it as well. She'd learned how to properly hunt in less than a week, much faster than Carter had learned.

"Do you remember what Mura said?" Sara asked as she finished her meal. Everyone was trying hard to forget the details of that day. Both boys were surprised at Sara for bringing it up. But they listened, hoping she picked up on some important information. "Do you really think Astrid is cursed?"

They considered this for a while. They had been so caught up with planning an attack and making sure Astrid was okay that they had forgotten about Mura saying Astrid was cursed. She'd never explained what the curse was though.

"Maybe we should ask her about it," Sara said after no one responded.

"Mura may have been lying," Grayson started. "Her whole new goal in life is to torture us. Maybe she said that so we would distrust Astrid and we would split apart."

"And if she is cursed, we have no idea why," Carter said. "This isn't a good time to jump to conclusions about anything."

Sara thought about this and then said, "Still, maybe we should ask her."

***

Duncan stood, feeling an intense mix of emotions: happiness, anger, confusion, excitement. He couldn't move. He just stared at the woman in front of him, who looked like his mother, but couldn't be.

Marcello and Astrid were equally confused. They knew Duncan's mother was dead, but he clearly thought that woman was her.

They stood to the side as Duncan began to walk toward the woman, his face frozen in disbelief.

"Hello, my son," whispered the still woman with a sweet smile on her face. She was not shocked. She was calm and ready, as if she had expected this moment to come.

Duncan leaped forward and wrapped his arms around her tight, a few uncontrollable tears falling from his eyes. Confusion didn't matter for the moment. Clearly, Duncan's mother stood before him, and that's all that mattered for now.

Paige began to pull away so she could look into Duncan's eyes. "What's going on?" he said, fighting back tears, his voice cracking. "Where's Dad? I thought you were dead." He gave her another tight hug.

She looked him in the eyes with a kind but serious gaze. "I am dead," she said with a sad smile.

Duncan stood back a bit, ready for answers. "What?" he asked in disbelief.

"My death was real," she said. "What you see and feel now is what's left of my spirit."

Astrid considered that for a second. *Okay*, she thought. *She's a ghost. I've seen ghosts before. But why is she here? Ghosts normally stay close to where they've died.* As she was about to ask the very question she was thinking, Paige continued her story.

"I didn't choose to be here," she said, trying to clarify what was going on. "These spell bookstores," she said, motioning to the building behind her, "are not run by the living. They're run by the spirits of Naturals who've died. It's not a choice. The magic chooses you when you die. However, you cannot leave. I must stay here, guarding the store, until another Natural is chosen, then I will finally move on to the afterlife.

"When I died, the darkness came. For what felt like days, there was nothing. Then, suddenly, I saw light. And then I was here. The woman who used to protect this place saw me. She smiled and said, 'You must be my replacement.' She then explained to me what I was and why I was here. Only Naturals are gifted with this secret."

She said this while looking directly at Astrid and Marcello. She was warning them. Only Naturals were supposed to know of the spirits who guarded the stores. So she was letting them know they'd better keep it a secret.

Duncan was speechless. The shock of seeing his mother was too much for him to handle. So Astrid asked the questions she figured Duncan would want the answers to. "Can you still use your magic?"

"Yes," Paige answered, turning to look at her son. "It's limited, though. I can only use it if it involves the protection of this store and its contents. I cannot contact anyone or leave this building."

"How long will you be here?" Astrid asked, thinking of the past guardian, Tina. She had been there for at least five hundred years.

"I don't know," she said, bothered by this fact. "It could be many years. It depends on when the next person who is chosen dies."

"So you can never leave?" Duncan finally asked, although it was more of a sad statement.

"No," she said. "I'm sorry. I wish I could have told you, but I can only communicate with those who come here."

Astrid looked up at the moon in the sky. Sometimes bookstore visits could take a long time, and they didn't want to waste a second since Mura's plans were completely unknown. "I don't mean to be *that* person," Astrid said, trying to get the situation moving, "but we're kind of in a rush. Maybe you could come back another day to chat with your mom. But right now, we need her help."

Duncan ignored Astrid for a moment. He suddenly didn't care about anything but spending time here with his mom. He didn't want to go back to Blessings, especially not after the other day.

Paige, however, could sense the urgency. She gave Astrid and Marcello an understanding nod and motioned Duncan into the building, closing the door behind her. Only Naturals were allowed inside, so Astrid and Marcello sat outside while they waited for an answer to be found.

***

The inside of the building was huge, with three large floors and a deep, wide basement below all filled with books. It was an exciting experience for Duncan. He had never been around so many spell books before, and this place had more than he could count.

He wanted to look at them all, learning all the spells. Although Naturals had different levels of strength, learning new spells increased the amount of magic they had. Duncan was strong for a Natural, but in some ways, that was useless since he knew very few spells. However, if he did begin to learn some, his magic would increase greatly. He was excited for that.

After Paige pried for a few minutes, trying to get Duncan to care again about the reason he came, he finally began to tell his mother why he had visited the bookstore. He explained the whole story, sparing no details, even the gruesome story of Mel and Astrid being tortured.

"This is bad," she finally said to him.

It wasn't the answer Duncan was expecting.

"Getting involved with vampires is dangerous, and often foolish. Naturals who get involved with vampires often die."

He began to wonder if maybe he shouldn't have told her the whole story. Maybe he should have just said he needed spell books since he had none. He couldn't help but tell her everything. He thought he had lost his mother forever, but there she stood in front of him. "It's a little too late for that, don't you think?" he said with a laugh.

"It's never too late," she answered, her face and tone serious.

Other Naturals walked around the store, leaving money or crystals on the counter as they walked out with books.

Duncan couldn't imagine not helping his friends. He wanted to listen to his mother, but he had to finish what he had started; maybe afterward, he'd stop helping vampires, but he couldn't stop yet. They'd probably all die without his help. And he wasn't sure he could ever escape Mura and Jazel.

"I have to help," he said. "The question is; will you help me?"

His mother smiled, placing her hand on his shoulder. Of course she would help.

She led him to a corner of the library and handed him three books. "The first book is the one you will need now," she said. "It has the spells you were looking for. The others are for when this mess is done. I wish I could help you with this. Jazel is not a Natural to be trifled with."

"I think it's too late to avoid her," Duncan said with a chuckle as he thought of Astrid nearly killing Jazel. "But thank you." They smiled at each other. They sat for a bit looking at the spells. Duncan decided to memorize a few before he left.

After talking for a bit, Duncan remembered why he had come and that he needed to leave.

"You'll have to come back sometime," Paige said.

Duncan wondered if Marcello would still be outside or not.

"I'm always here."

Duncan opened the door, armed with a few more spells and three books filled with plenty more. He looked back at his mother, still unable to find words for just how grateful he felt to have reunited with her. The idea that he might receive the formal training he craved floated around in his head, and he looked into her eyes with a gentle smile. He pulled the door open fully and felt a sudden rush of heat-filled air, smoke billowing into the entrance. Flames surrounded the building, dancing just on the other side of the protective barrier around the shop. The smell nearly choked him. His mother grabbed his arm, pulling him inside, but he clung to the edge, scanning everywhere for his friends. They were nowhere in sight.

Chapter 16

Paige pushed her son back into the building, shutting the door behind her. "What are you doing?" Duncan shouted. "The building is going to burn!"

Paige began to gather the few people in the building, while Duncan stood nervously, worried for his friends and himself.

"The building won't burn," his mother said as the Naturals all gathered together. "It's bound by a very powerful spell," she said, looking at Duncan. "Not even Jazel could break it."

Duncan ran to the window, ignoring his mother, trying to decide his next plan of action. He hoped his friends weren't outside. But as he looked out the window, he couldn't see anything past the flames except one man.

He stood far away from the building, keeping a safe distance between himself and the flames. His eyes were cold, and he looked directly at Duncan. The intensity of the man's stare gave Duncan the urge to turn away. But he kept looking, hoping to get some answers from this man's eyes.

He turned to tell his mother about the man outside, but she was busy doing something he had never seen before. The Naturals in the room all held hands as Paige whispered some spell under her breath, her eyes closed. He had a strange feeling though; he felt strong. The room was filled with energy. He could even see the other Naturals glowing slightly. He felt the energy all over his body.

Duncan looked back out the window and saw the flames were out. Paige's eyes opened, and she rushed to the window to see if her spell had worked. "There's a man outside," Duncan called loudly. But as he glanced outside, the man was gone. Astrid and Marcello's car still stood outside, a little burnt from the flames.

Worry rushed through his body. *Where did he go?* he wondered, thinking about the mysterious man.

His mother closed her eyes again, trying to sense whatever presences might have been outside. "I think the man you saw is gone," she said, still looking cautiously out the window, scanning for any signs of life or movement. "Your friends are gone too."

She looked at her son, whose face was tight and worried. The other Naturals in the room began to whisper, confused as to why the building was attacked. So, to protect her son and encourage the others to return, she lied. "It happens sometimes," she said plainly. "Some other supernatural creatures know of these libraries, and they come to terrorize the Naturals inside. It's probably best if everyone went home now, though, just in case."

The Naturals looked suspicious but relieved the place was no longer covered in flames. They all said their separate goodbyes and individually disappeared into thin air, teleporting back to their homes. One of the spells Duncan had learned that night was a teleportation spell. If his friends didn't come back, it looked like he might have to use it.

"Come over here," his mother called from across the room. As he walked over, she pulled a blank piece of paper from a drawer and placed it on a large wooden table. She waved her hand over it a few times, and each time, a new map appeared on the page.

"Wow," Duncan said to himself. New spells never stopped amazing him.

Finally, Paige stopped on one specific map. Duncan looked at it closely as a strange black dot appeared. She waved her hand a few more times, this time whispering something to herself, although the map didn't change. Then, two more dots appeared: one was black and the other was white, although at first, it appeared red, changing colors shortly after it showed up.

"Interesting," his mother said.

"What is this?" Duncan asked.

"Well, the dots represent the location of people I'm looking for," she said, pointing to the first black dot that appeared. "This is the man you saw outside. The black color means he is a vampire. These other two dots are your friends. Apparently, they're close; either they're being followed or he is." Then, the dots disappeared.

"What happened?" Duncan said, touching the map, hoping they would return.

"They're too fast," his mom said, looking at her son. "If a vampire is running, the map can't keep up. However, at least we know they're alive."

"So, the white dot must mean hunter then," he said, excited to learn new details about his magic and also happy to know his friends were alive. Knowing them, they were chasing the vampire who probably torched the outside of the store.

"Well, that's actually what's interesting," his mom answered. "I've never seen a white dot appear. I don't actually know what it means. At first, the color I expected appeared: red, for supernatural hunters. But then, it changed to white. She does have a strange energy about her."

Duncan looked quickly at his mother. "I felt that too," he said, surprised. "When we first met, I didn't trust her because of that weird energy. But, after what has happened the past few days, I've come to ignore that feeling."

Paige looked at the map, curious about Astrid and the strange white color that had appeared. She wanted to research in some of the books and see if she could find an answer. But she shook her head. They had more important things to do.

"I want your help with a spell," she said, walking over to the other side of the table. "According to this map, your friends are rather close. I can't use my spells to help them, but I can use a spell on the other vampire since he was probably involved with the fire outside. I want to temporarily paralyze him. But I need your help to reach him."

Duncan nodded in agreement, excited to be a part of the in-depth spell. Paige reached over and held his hand. "I'm going to be casting the spell," she said, looking at him seriously. "But I need you to think hard about the face of the man we're looking for. I want you to focus your energy in the palm of your hand."

She touched her finger to the middle of his palm, holding it there. "Focus all of your energy here," she said. She closed her eyes and began to recite the spell. Duncan did as he was told; he focused on the man's face and sent his energy and magic to the palm of his hand. He felt powerful sharing his magic with his mother. Suddenly, in his mind, he saw the vampire, but not just the image he was creating. It was the actual vampire, falling to the ground. Within seconds, Astrid and Marcello were on him, and his mother stopped the spell. They had succeeded in paralyzing him.

***

"What the fuck?" Astrid said as she looked at the mysterious vampire motionless on the ground. His eyes were open, but he wasn't moving. "What happened to him?" she said, walking cautiously around him.

"If I had to guess," Marcello started, "I would say this is the work of a Natural, probably Duncan and Paige."

Astrid gave the motionless body a little nudge. "Yeah, I guess he's just stuck," she said in a very proud tone, although she hadn't done anything but chase him for a while. "Now what?" she asked, looking at Marcello.

He gave her an unsure look.

They didn't know if they should kill him or take him back to Blessings. They also weren't sure how long he'd be frozen.

The main concern was the vampire's strength. From his speed, Marcello and Astrid thought he might old, which meant he was powerful. Thick, metal chains could often keep vampires still, but some of the older vampires could break the metal. Assuming the vampire was connected to Mura, it would make more sense that he was young since Astrid had killed all of her evil family back in the eighties. She considered maybe he was just extremely fast for a young vampire. But they decided he needed to come back with them to Blessings.

To keep him weakened, Astrid stuck two stakes through his sides and two in his legs. She wasn't really one for torturing people, but they needed to see if he had any answers. After the stakes were placed, Marcello lifted the vampire up and ran as fast as he could back to Blessings. Astrid ran back to Duncan.

***

Only a few minutes after casting their spell, they heard a knock on the door. Paige touched her son on the shoulder, signaling him to stay where he was. She was already dead, so she should open the door. If someone malicious was at the door, they couldn't hurt or kill her.

She opened the door slowly, looking through as quickly as she could. To her relief, Astrid stood at the door, smiling.

"Did you catch him?" Paige asked as Duncan made his way over to the door.

"You mean the vampire who tried to burn this place down?" Astrid said playfully. "He has been rendered powerless, thanks to you and me, and Marcello is taking him back to Blessings. How long will he be paralyzed?"

"A few hours," Paige answered. "Are you sure it is safe to keep him alive?"

"Probably not," Astrid answered honestly. "But we need to talk to him. And, I hate to rush you, but after everything that has happened, are you ready to go? We need to get back ASAP."

"He's ready," Paige said, giving her son a proud smile. They had never performed a spell together before, but Duncan did a flawless job of helping her.

Duncan ran back to the table and picked up his three new spell books. Paige and Duncan gave each other a hug, and Duncan promised he would return soon. They had so many more things to talk about. Astrid looked around and saw the car was a half chard mess. She looked at Duncan. "Have any teleportation spells up your sleeve now?" she asked.

He shook his head no. But Paige lifted her hand over one of his spell books and it opened in his arms to a page with teleportation spell. Astrid glanced at the book for no reason at all. She couldn't see the words on the pages. Only Naturals could read and understand the ancient words. It comes to them naturally.

Duncan scanned the book page, then reached over and grab Astrid's hand. He smiled. "You ready?" he asked.

"Born ready," she teased. Duncan focused his attention, read the words and they vanished off into the night.

***

Carter, Grayson, and Sara heard a knock on the door, although it was quickly followed by the sound of someone entering. They all rushed to the door, fangs out, ready to attack. A strange thing happens though; Sara jumped in front of the boys, as if protecting them. Her fangs shown and she growled under her breath. Grayson and Carter were taken aback and looked suspiciously at one another.

They didn't completely relax, even when they saw Marcello, because he wasn't alone. Resting on his shoulder was a wounded, motionless, vampire. "Do you have any thick chains or handcuffs?" Marcello asked in a super normal tone.

"Uh, no," Carter answered, confused. "Who's this guy?"

"Not sure," Marcello answered, "but he tried to burn down the spell bookstore, so we're assuming he's an enemy. He's currently paralyzed, but I'm not sure for how long."

"He's bleeding," Sara said, with everyone still standing and staring at Marcello and the body he carried. The all returned to their normal stances, but Sara had a glint in her eye that made Marcello nervous. But he didn't have time to dwell on that thought.

"He's been staked to keep him weak," Marcello said. "We're not sure how strong he is so need to keep him detained. I'm going back to my house. We have some chains that may hold him."

The vampires found it strange Marcello and Astrid would keep restraints and chains in their home. But then again, she *was* a vampire hunter.

"We'll come with you," Carter said, walking toward the door.

Marcello didn't object. He was just about to tell them they needed to come with him. The sun would be up in just a little bit. He would have to go to sleep, leaving this paralyzed vampire with Carter and his friends. It would be better if other people were there to watch him. Hopefully, Duncan and Astrid would be home soon. She was a much faster driver than Marcello was.

They all ran over to Marcello's house by the little pond. When they arrived, Sara quickly sent Duncan a text to inform him of their new location. He didn't reply, although Marcello insisted he was probably asleep. It had been a long night and, although Duncan was a Natural, his needs were much like a human—and he was definitely low on sleep.

Marcello laid the still vampire on the floor of his living room and went downstairs to grab a few things. He returned with a heavy wooden chair and thick metal chains. He wrapped the vampire tightly, making sure to confine his feet and tie his hands behind his back.

They were all a little worried about the vampire being inside the house. Last time they brought a vampire inside to question her, she turned out to be a Natural in disguise. But they needed to take the risk.

Just as Marcello clasped the metal lock around the chains, life returned to the confined vampire. He yelled loudly and fought hard to get out of the chains. But the weakening from the stakes and confinement of the chains was too much. After a few minutes, he was still—but his eyes were filled with life and rage.

Chapter 17

Marcello stepped back, looking at the awake vampire. He didn't speak, just sat there, still and angry.

"Do you want to tell us your name?" Carter asked, looking cautiously at the vampire. He was silent, but he stared hard at Sara, while also scanning the faces of the room, as if looking for someone else.

Marcello was about to take over the conversation when his eyes began to get heavy. He looked out the window as the light of the sun started to tint the air with dark purples and pinks. He wondered if the other vampire was a day-walker or not.

The bound vampire's eyes looked sleepier too. His strength was starting to disappear, and he looked cautiously outside, just as Marcello had. The other vampires noticed too, although they could walk in the sun. At the same time, they all reached into their pockets, pulled out individual little vials, and dropped a small drop of whatever liquid was inside on their tongues, carefully placing the vial back where they were done. Marcello realized that must be the potion they used to walk in the day.

Grayson noticed his look and said, "I'm sure Duncan could make one for you too. Then you wouldn't be controlled by the sun."

Marcello shook his head and said, "I haven't seen the sun in so many years. Honestly, I don't even miss it."

"Keep it in mind, though," Grayson added, "in case you ever change your mind."

Marcello gave him a smile but then looked cautiously at all the open windows.

"We need to cover the windows," Marcello said. He ran quickly upstairs and was back down in a few seconds. He had all the sheets, blankets, and towels that he owned. He headed over to the kitchen to start there. They all spread out around the downstairs, covering the windows to make sure no light came in.

In a way, it was a great scenario. Although Marcello would need to sleep, so would the tied-up vampire. And even if he chose not to sleep, he would be very weak during the day. But Carter, Sara, and Grayson could all stay awake during the day to watch him.

After the windows were all closed, Marcello made his way to the stairs.

"Where are you going?" Grayson asked, a little worried to be left alone with the mysterious vampire.

"I have to sleep," Marcello answered. The sun was almost over the horizon. The windows were covered well, so he wasn't worried about their guest frying in the light. "I think he does too. If you need anything, just call, loudly. Since all the windows are covered, I can help as long as we stay in the house." And with that, he was gone upstairs, in his room, and fast asleep.

The vampire sat there, still staring at Sara, although the intensity had diminished. He needed sleep, but it looked like he was going to try and fight through it, his eyes looking heavy.

Not too much longer after Marcello had gone to sleep, Astrid and Duncan unexpectedly appeared right inside the front door. This took Carter, Sara, and Grayson by surprise.

Astrid ran fast to the kitchen sink and vomited. Everyone, including Duncan, were confused. After a moment, she came back in the room and took a few deep breaths, then stare at the captive as if nothing had happened. "Oh yes, we have a guest."

"What happen to you?" Carter asked, a little worried about Astrid, but also curious.

"Oh," Astrid said with a chuckle, "Teleportation does not settle well with me."

"Teleportation?" Carter said allowed.

"Yes! We used a teleportation spell!" Duncan said excitedly. "I may never walk anywhere ever again."

Sara walked over and gave both of them a smile. "Glad you two are safe," she said, relieved her friends were home. They all looked over at the vampire, who was still awake and staring at them.

"He looks pissed," Duncan said as he decided to keep a safe distance from him.

The tied-up vampire shifted his focus from Sara to Astrid. Intensity returned to his eyes. And finally, he decided to speak.

"I've never met a hunter who was friends with vampires before," he said, with a devious look on his face.

It made everyone in the room uncomfortable, but not Astrid. She was used to vampires trying to be intimidating.

"Well, since you're still alive, I'm guessing you've never been kidnapped by a hunter, either," she said as she walked over to him. He watched her carefully as she came over. She grabbed a chair from the dining room table and sat in it near her unidentified captive.

"First time for everything, I guess," he answered, his face in a state of bitterness. "Have you ever had to kill the vampires you have befriended?" He was trying to make her angry. But those were things she'd heard before.

"I've never really been friends with many other vampires, other than Marcello," she answered, giving a glance toward the upstairs, "so, no. I tend not to befriend vampires who need to be killed. So I wouldn't count on us being friends."

His eyes narrowed, although a small smile crept on his face. If anything, at least Astrid could stand her ground.

"I know a few things about you, you know," he said, beginning to struggle over the pain of the stakes in his body.

Astrid tensed. She knew what he probably meant: her curse. And, although Sara, Grayson, and Carter had heard Mura mention it, she didn't want to talk about it.

"Well, that's good," Astrid said, trying to change the subject. "Why is it Jazel has not made you a day-walker?"

He laughed. He knew Astrid was avoiding what he might say. "It must be terrible to only have those who hate you remember who you are," he said, his words piercing through Astrid's heart. "I do wonder, though, why is it, year after year, Marcello still remembers who you are? Are you sure he actually cares about you?"

With those words, Astrid jabbed a stake through his heart. "Fucking vampires," she whispered under her breath. Her patience had been used up on him. Her talking mood was gone. She knew there would be ramifications for killing Mura's protégé, but she didn't care.

Everyone in the room stood back, worried about what Astrid was going to do next. She ripped the stake back out from his chest, dropping it on the floor and watching his body turn to ash. She knew it wasn't helpful to kill him, but no one was allowed to talk about her curse except her. And it was rare she wanted to talk about it.

The eyes in the room focused on Astrid. She looked around at them, those vampires. She felt conflicted. Maybe she should have never helped them, never tried to be friends with them. He was right. Soon she would die, this curse cycle would be over, and these people standing in the room would no longer remember her. No matter what she did, soon, she wouldn't even be a memory to them.

Without another word, she ran out the door. No one knew where she was going. All, but Carter just stood there, confused. He ran out after her, but after only a few seconds he had lost track her. God she was fast.

He came back in, defeated and worried. They all stared at the dead body on the ground. Sara was the one to speak up. "Maybe she isn't the good guy?" she questioned.

"Don't say that" Carter insisted, looking unsurely at the pile of ash before him.

"But she seems to have no regard for any vampire's life," she said. "Are we sure we should continue to trust her? What if we are the next ones to get staked?"

"Shut up!" Carter shouted at Sara. But she barely flinched as a smug look crawled across her face knowing she had put some doubt into his mind. But Marcello, who had heard Astrid come home and was listening, had heard what Sara said. Carter walked over to the open door and looked longingly at the morning sun. He sighed. "Let's just go home."

Sara dropped her smug look and grabbed Grayson's hand with a smile and they all went back to their house, discussing the events from the day. They kept repeating the words, "Those who hate you remember who you are." They didn't understand, though their curiosity was highly piqued.

Carter worried about Astrid. He wanted to talk to her. She had done so much for them, and he couldn't imagine that any curse could keep him from wanting to be friends with her. Curse or no curse, he felt connected to her. And he wanted that connection to grow.

As the sun disappeared over the horizon, Marcello showed up at Carter's house. And without knocking on their door, he once again just let himself inside. "Where is Astrid?" he asked, worried and confused. "I saw the vampire ash, but everyone was gone when I awoke. What happened?"

They looked at each other, unsure how to answer the question. "We don't know where she went," Carter finally answered. "The vampire started saying things Astrid didn't like. So she killed him and ran out the door." Marcello looked concerned.

"He mentioned a curse," Sara said, and Marcello looked mad. He turned around to leave, but Carter ran up and stopped him.

"Wait!" Carter said, not wanting Marcello to leave. "Where are you going?"

"To find Astrid," Marcello answered, looking like he might attack Carter.

"I want to come with you," Carter said, a serious look in his eyes. Marcello didn't seem convinced. "Please, let me help you find her."

He stared at Carter for a moment, deciding if he wanted his help or not. "I know where she is," Marcello answered.

"Where?" Carter asked, confused about how he suddenly knew her location.

"She's at Willow Manor," he said.

"What!" Carter asked, shocked. "Why would she go there alone?"

"Because she's angry," Marcello said. "I'm going there now. You can join if you want, but I'm not responsible for what may happen there." He moved around Carter and stepped back through the door. He looked back for just a second to see if anyone would join him. To his surprise, everyone stepped forward. Although, Sara had an unsure look on her face.

"I can get us all there in a few seconds," Duncan said, referring to his teleportation spell. "That way, we can still surprise them by showing up inside the manor."

Marcello smiled. "Let's go then."

Duncan told them to all hold hands, and he began to whisper a spell to himself. They all closed their eyes when he said to, and when they opened them, they were standing in the same room where they had watched Mel get tortured to death. Her body still lay their mangled. Duncan shivers. Seeing Mel was not only a shock, but he remembered being with Astrid while she was tortured.

For a moment, they were still, taking in the room and building around them. But they all had the same unusual feeling: emptiness. They couldn't sense anyone inside the building. As they looked around the room more, they noticed a real emptiness. Things were gone; furniture, pictures, mirrors, all missing. Suspicion ran through their bodies.

They made their way toward the door quietly, still worried someone might be inside. But as they opened the door, they saw no one, just the same empty appearance of the house.

They decided to split up: Marcello and Duncan went one way together, while the other vampires stayed in their group. But to their surprise, all they found were smells and trash of things left behind. Marcello and Duncan even stumbled upon a secret basement room, but even that was barren and empty. All that was left was the smell of old blood.

They all met back up at the front of the house, confused but relieved to find no one there. "I wonder if they took Astrid with them wherever they went," Carter asked, not as relaxed as his friends were. He was worried about Astrid.

They suddenly heard a strange sound outside. They all stood still and silent as they listened.

They heard it again. "It sounds like rocks," Grayson said, his ear turned toward the door. This time, when they heard the sound, the vampires could clearly make out what it was. Someone was picking up rocks and throwing them outside. They realized they weren't alone.

They all cautiously walked over to the front door. The empty manor gave off an even more ominous feel than when it was filled with vampires.

Carter opened the door, and Marcello looked out as it opened. A wave of relief fell over his face. He pushed the door the rest of the way, causing Carter to lose his balance. He looked at the girl sitting on the stairs and smiled as she said, "I was wondering how long you guys would look around."

Astrid was sitting on the front porch, doing just as they had heard: picking up rocks from the gravel sidewalk and tossing them effortlessly back onto the ground. "I heard you when you got here," she said, still looking at the ground.

"You could have come to say you were okay," Carter said, which caught Astrid off guard. She expected Marcello to be the one to say something.

"I figured it would be better if you discovered for yourself," she said, turning her body to look at everyone. "The place is dead and empty. They're completely gone. I searched a mile radius around the whole place and couldn't find any sign of them."

Astrid was sad. Her face was plain. She had come here, ready to kill, and instead, she was greeted with silence. She didn't even have to fight anyone.

Marcello gave her a smile, happy to see her okay. She managed a measly little grin. Carter came and sat next to her. "So what should we do now?" he asked, giving her a very friendly smile.

She looked deep into his eyes, trying to read his thoughts. She took a deep breath. He was close to her on these stairs, looking so sweetly into her eyes. His smell filled her thoughts. She felt happy and relaxed with him next to her.

She gave a quick glance to Marcello, and he nodded while they had a conversation without words.

"I think what I should do now is tell you about my curse."

Chapter 18

Astrid raced through the woods, running for her life. If they caught her, she wouldn't be killed, but her life would definitely be over. She had on a long white cotton dress that swirled as she ran over the thick snow. Dirt and water covered the expensive fabric. Her feet were bare and almost blue from the cold. She had been running all day, her body scraped and bruised from tripping over nearly invisible branches. There were also signs she had been attacked, such as two black eyes.

The sun was down, but she didn't stop running. Thirst, hunger, and exhaustion were beginning to set in. She had been starved the few days before she found the moment to run. But at that time, the idea of freedom kept her going.

As she sprinted, she was losing hope. There was nothing for miles, and she couldn't stop. When she did, she heard the sound of men and horses not too far behind her. The thick trees had made it hard for the horses to navigate, which was the only reason she hadn't been caught yet. She cursed the snow for leaving behind her tracks wherever she stepped.

She was running from her husband, a rich noble ruling a small kingdom near the Tiber River. To Astrid, he was more of a tyrant than a man.

She had been forced to marry him only a few months before, and since then, she had only lived in hell. That man was sadistic, torturing Astrid, his wife, for the fun of it. He didn't care when she screamed or cried, or that she had no love for him at all. He wanted her, and he took her. She had no choice in the matter.

The only reason she had stayed as long as she did was for her family. As a noble's wife, her family was given money and food, something they didn't always have. But she couldn't take it anymore.

He had begun lending her out to his guards and friends. She was nothing but a toy, a trophy, and a punching bag to her new husband. Astrid had had enough. She'd tried to run a few days' prior but was caught. That was when she learned to leave in the morning, not during the night. She would rather die than live another day as his slave.

With the sun no longer up, she worried more that she would be caught or injure herself in the darkness. She couldn't feel her feet anymore. Although, by the moonlight, she saw blood in her tracks.

She fell more, unable to see large logs and branches down in front of her. The moon was bright, but she needed more light. She knew she wasn't going to last much longer. She was too tired, too cold, and her body was suffering from dehydration and serious malnutrition. The elements would soon get to her.

Suddenly, she heard the sound of a wild animal. She didn't choose to stop, but something grabbed her entire body, pushing her hard against a tree.

She didn't tense up, and she didn't fight. She couldn't. She used the only fight she had left in her to run, and she was finally still. She felt pressure on her arms and the warm breath of the creature that had her. It felt like a person holding her there, but the strength was too great.

In her exhaustion, she looked up at whatever, or whoever, held her. His bright-green eyes glowed in the moonlight. His hair was disheveled, but his face was confused and curious.

Even in the dark, she could see who was holding her. She knew those eyes and that face. And she could tell he remembered her.

"Marcello?" she whispered, but her eyes closed. When she realized it was him, she relaxed and let go. Her body gave up. And what she didn't know then was that she died in his arms.

***

Less than an hour later, she awoke, lying in the snow. She felt strange. A sharp pain rushed through her body. She couldn't breathe for a moment because of how strong the pain was. When it was gone, she was relieved, but only for an instant.

Then, her skin was on fire. It rushed through her body, and she lay on the ground, convulsing while her back arched beyond its normal range and she reached desperately for some comfort around her. It lasted a while. She didn't think of Marcello, or getting caught, or anything. The agony consumed her thoughts.

After a few hours, Astrid lay motionless on the ground. The pain was gone, but what was left was strange. She felt strong. Her energy had returned. She was taken aback by the odd glow everything had. At first, she thought it was morning. But the stars in the sky said otherwise. Somehow, she could see in the dark.

An unfamiliar smell filled her senses, one she would get very used to: the smell of blood. It wasn't hers, but there was certainly a lot. She stood up from her place on the ground, looking around, trying to find the smell's location.

And then she saw the bodies. At least a few dozen lay cold on the ground; a few horses and dogs were dead with them. She wondered what had killed them all. A strange jolt of happiness rushed through her body as she saw the man responsible for her anguish lying dead on the ground. She had no husband to find her.

She felt no grief for the bodies on the ground, just overwhelming pride that he would send so many men to find her, and overwhelming happiness that they were all dead.

Behind her, she heard someone breathing. She turned quickly, much faster than she expected, and saw again her old friend standing near her, his face and body covered in blood. But she wasn't scared.

"Did you kill them?" she asked, not a hint of fear in her eyes, just curiosity.

"Yes," he answered, looking straight at his new creation and the girl he had left to protect years ago. "Do you know what you are?"

"Yes," she said. "I'm free."

When Astrid was sixteen, she was set to be wed to someone she deeply cared about: her best friend since she could remember, Marcello. He was three years older than her, but she had a maturity and spunk no one could resist.

Although she didn't love Marcello as she thought one should love a husband, she cared about him deeply. They were best friends, not lovers, but they would accept marriage over losing each other.

But on the day of their wedding, Marcello was nowhere to be found. And Astrid was heartbroken.

She searched for days, trying to find him or even a trace of where he had gone. But after realizing she could not search for him, she just sat around, hoping he would come back.

But he never did. However, she finally knew why.

The night before their wedding, on his way home, Marcello had been attacked and fatally wounded by thieves. He lay there, dying on the ground, when a strange woman approached him. Although she took away his life, she gave him back another one, a better one. And that was what Marcello had done to Astrid.

"You're a vampire," he said. "You're strong, and fast, and nearly indestructible. But there's a price."

Before he could finish, she spoke. "I can no longer sit in the sun, and I must drink blood to survive," she said.

Marcello looked at her in disbelief. He didn't understand how she could know such things.

"When I was a child," she started, "strange creatures— vampires, werewolves, Naturals—would come by my house at night. I don't know why they wanted to talk to me, or what drew them there, but I know what a vampire is. I know what I can do."

Suddenly, Marcello was concerned. There was a fire in her eyes that he hadn't seen in a vampire before. She looked like a wild, hungry animal.

He reached for her arm, ready to calm her down, tell her she needed to learn control of her abilities.

But before his hand could touch her, she shifted away, giving him a devious smile, and vanished into the night.

He searched for months, trying to catch her. But she was fast, much faster than a normal newborn vampire. All he found were the bodies she left behind. There were hundreds. She would go into a town and kill whole large families. He knew he had to find her. He had created her, and it was his responsibility to control his creation.

As the months went on, her killing sprees only got worse; she began to kill entire villages, leaving not one drop of blood left behind her. Marcello became desperate. He found a few vampire friends and begged for their help in finding her.

With their assistance, about eight months after he created her, he was finally able to catch her.

He put her in an underground chamber, chaining her up tightly and putting a stake in each leg. She screamed and growled for days, fighting like a beast to free herself. But she was fast, she wasn't strong enough to break the chains.

After being starved, staked, and chained up for a month, she finally began to use words, and the fire in her eyes began to die out.

A few days later, he gave her food and released her from her chains. But this time, she didn't run. She stayed beside Marcello as a tamer and reasonable vampire, waiting for his next order. Unfortunately, it was too late.

As they exited the chamber, a strange woman waited for them outside. Her eyes were white and angry. At a closer glance, Astrid realized she wasn't standing on the ground, but floating a few inches above it. She knew the woman must be a Natural, and she didn't look happy.

"Do you know why I'm here?" she asked, her voice sounding like three different voices.

Marcello stood in front of Astrid, trying to keep her protected. "No," he admitted. "But I'm sure whatever it is, we can talk about it."

"Do you remember this woman?" As she said this, a strange image appeared in the air. It was a woman, but she wasn't solid. It looked like they could put their hand straight through her, like a reflection in the water.

Astrid stepped out from behind Marcello. She knew who the woman was. "Yes," she answered, staying strong and holding her ground. Suddenly, Marcello flew twenty feet across the forest floor, and the woman came only inches away from Astrid's face.

"Do you remember killing her?" the Natural growled.

"Unfortunately, I do," Astrid answered, sure the woman would know if she was lying. "But I'm not the vampire I used to be."

Rage filled the Natural's eyes. "No," she said. "You are not. And you never will be again. You killed the woman I loved, and I will make sure you always remember that."

The Natural flew back, and the clouds began to cover the sky. Astrid couldn't move and Marcello was struggling to stand up. Fear rushed through their bodies.

The Natural began to speak the language of magic, using words Astrid did not know. But she knew it was bad. She felt pressure all over her body as if something were trying to press her flat. She fell to the ground, finding it difficult to handle the pain. A swirl of wind, leaves, and dust surrounded her body. She looked up only to see what appeared to be a funnel of clouds coming down from the sky right over her.

And although the Natural was speaking the words of magic, in Astrid's mind, the Natural spoke separate words to her.

"You will always know love," Astrid heard in her mind, "but it will always be taken from you. When you remember, they will forget. You will hunt the creatures that killed my love, and when you die, the cycle will start over again. Forever."

In an instant, the funnel surrounded Astrid's body, and a light flashed all around her. And then she was gone.

Astrid lay dead on the ground. Marcello desperately came over and held her close to himself. Suddenly, her body vanished into nothing. But what Marcello didn't know at the time was that it wasn't the last time he'd see Astrid.

Chapter 19

Almost sixteen years later, a beautiful girl named Kara was gathering water by the stream for her family. The next day was her sixteenth birthday, and her mother was planning on making a special meal for her. Her family didn't have much money, but they had a lot of love.

As she returned back to the house, she opened the door to find her mother putting out the fire for the night. She took the water buckets from Kara and gave her a big hug and kiss goodnight. Kara went off to the room that she and her sister shared.

She hopped in bed, closed her eyes, and fell asleep fast, thinking about the delicious meal her mother would make in the morning. But the moment midnight came and went, and her sixteenth birthday began, a wave of images flew through Kara's mind, shocking her awake and throwing her out of the bed.

She hit the floor hard. She sat there for a second, taking deep breaths, holding her aching head. *What just happened?* she thought to herself. And then she remembered it all. She remembered her real name: Astrid. She remembered her first family, her evil husband, her vampire-induced killing spree, and she remembered Marcello.

Her fall had woken her sister up, who moved over to see what the sound was on the other side of the bed. Astrid called from the floor, "I'm okay." But unexpectedly, her sister screamed.

Astrid stood up fast. "What's wrong?" she asked, moving over to try to calm her sister.

"Help!" her sister screamed. "Someone's in the house."

Astrid stood, confused. She looked behind her. She wondered who her sister was talking about. Then, her mother and father entered the room. Her mother backed away while her dad carried a large axe in his hand. "Get out of this house!" her father screamed. She didn't understand what was going on.

"Dad, what are you doing?" Astrid asked, a few tears welling up in her eyes.

He lifted his axe, ready to attack, and instinctively, Astrid ran out the open window. She stopped outside, confused and hurt. She didn't know what was going on. Why did her family just try to kill her?

Her dad came out the door, axe still in hand. "Go away now!" he yelled, moving toward Astrid.

"Don't you remember me?" she asked, tears streaming down her face.

"Did you not hear me?" he screamed. "Get off my land!"

This time, she turned her face and ran away as quickly as she could. A few seconds later, she stopped; she was running as fast as a vampire. She had made it a mile down the river in a few seconds.

She balled up her fist and punched a large tree growing by the river; it shattered and fell to the ground. She sat on the ground, tears rushing down her warm face. *What's going on?* she thought, confused.

Then, she thought about what the Natural had said to her. "You will always know love, but it will always be taken from you. When you remember, they will forget. You will hunt the creatures that killed my love, and when you die, the cycle will start over again. Forever."

She thought about it all night, realizing that when she remembered her past, her family seemed to forget all about her. "When you remember, they will forget."

She felt sick, lying there on the ground. She missed both her families: the one she left years ago when she got married, and the one she'd just lost. And she missed Marcello. It made her sad to think about him. She would never see him again, and if she did, he probably wouldn't remember her.

She realized she did this to herself. She had let the initial power and hunger of being a vampire take control of her. She killed so many people. Maybe she deserved it.

Thinking she was a vampire, Astrid sat up all night, thinking of her curse, her family, and her sadness. She didn't take cover when the sun began to rise. She was going to let it take her. She deserved to feel the burn of the light.

But as the sun made its way over the horizon, all she felt was the pleasant warmth of the light. She didn't burn, and she didn't have a craving for blood: she was thirsty for water and hungry for food. *Maybe I'm not a vampire.*

***

Everyone had listened intensely to Astrid's story.

She then explained the little details she learned throughout the two thousand years she'd been cursed. For one, people who loved her never remembered who she was. However, if someone developed a dislike for her or hated her, they would remember her forever.

The cycle went like this: Astrid was born, always looking the different, to a family who always loved and cared for her more than most families would. If she had friends, they were always very close friends who also cared deeply for her. But, when she turned sixteen, everyone forgot who she was, and she regained her memory, including all the lives she'd lived before. And she changed physically and looked like she did in her first life as the original Astrid. Then, the day she turned twenty-five, she died a painful, agonizing death. And the next day, she was reborn, growing up once again in a loving home. She came to realize her curse was known as the hunter's curse. She never saw the Natural again who put the curse on her, though she swore she could sometimes feel her cold eyes watching her.

She and Marcello had tried many times to break the curse, consulting multiple Naturals and supernatural beings. But they all seem to have the same answer, which is that curses had to be broken by the one who cast them.

The worst part about the curse was the moment she regained her memory. When it happened, it was literally a painful experience. She remembered all the people she loved who no longer cared for her or even remembered her. The emotional pain was harder to bear than any of the physical pain she had endured in her long life.

"But how does Marcello remember who you are?" Sara asked.

It was an interesting question because Astrid didn't really have an answer.

"Honestly," she started, "I'm not sure. The first time I regained my memory, I hadn't seen Marcello in sixteen years. I was sure he would have forgotten me, but since I had nothing else to do, I went to look for him. I wasn't a very good hunter yet, so it took eight years to find him. But then, one night, I saw him, just walking through Rome. I went up to him, expecting him to have no idea who I was, but when he saw me, he picked me up and held me tight in his arms. I felt such a relief knowing he remembered me."

Unfortunately, their time together was short. Astrid was twenty-four when she found Marcello. She didn't know about the cycles of her curse yet, so when she turned twenty-five, she suddenly died and disappeared, leaving Marcello alone again.

That time, he stayed in Rome, hoping Astrid would return. Every night for sixteen years, he wandered up and down the streets, just waiting for her to find him again. Then one day, she appeared. When she regained her memory, she went back to the last place she had seen Marcello. It was a long shot, but she had to start somewhere. To her surprise, he was still there. And he still remembered.

The next time she died, she and Marcello had made a plan to meet at a certain bar in Italy they had visited. After the last two cycles, she guessed she would be there in sixteen years. And sure enough, she wasn't late for their meeting.

"I don't really care why Marcello remembers me," Astrid said. "I'm just really happy he does. It may be because he created me when I first became a vampire, or maybe the Natural made it so he would remember. Who knows, really?"

Then, Carter asked the question he was dreading to ask. "So how old are you now?"

Astrid's face went solemn. Although she needed to tell them, she didn't want to. Since she had explained her curse, the oncoming end of her current cycle seemed much bleaker, especially since she'd made friends.

"I have less than three months left," she said sadly. Although she looked older than sixteen, when Astrid regained her memory, she stopped aging. So, to everyone else, Astrid looked like she could still be in her late teens, maybe close to twenty. "I'm cursed, and it's because I was a bad person. But I can assure you, that person died two thousand years ago."

They all were in shock, something that had happened a lot in the past few days.

Carter placed an arm around her and whispered, "I don't think we will ever forget you." Astrid smiled, her eyes filling ever so slightly with water. She was worried her story would be greeted with hate, but instead, it was greeted with acceptance. Once again, she was even sadder she only had three months left to live.

***

The group left the Willow Manor and returned together to Carter and Grayson's home. Since Mura and her family were nowhere to be found, they weren't sure what to do. Astrid was the best vampire hunter there was, but since the Willow family had a powerful Natural on their side, their tracks could easily be hidden.

They all sat around the rest of the night, talking and eating, the vampires drinking blood bags from Marcello's stash. He decided not to mention it was mostly Astrid's renewable blood. Duncan shared his food with Astrid, though he kept to himself. Not distant and cautious, just deep in thought, like he was planning something. The only one who was suspicious of his silence was Sara, mainly because she knew what he was probably thinking.

Before daylight set in, Astrid and Marcello returned to their home to sleep, although Carter tried to persuade Astrid to rest at their house for the day. But with a kind smile, she resisted. She wanted to be home with Marcello, just in case they had any unwanted visitors.

Astrid had officially become a night owl after all of their late nights. It made her a little sad knowing she wouldn't be finishing the classes she had just started.

As she and Marcello left, Grayson and Carter went upstairs to sleep. Grayson motioned for Sara to join him, and she said she would soon. Right then, she wanted to talk to Duncan, who was still sitting alone, thinking to himself downstairs.

She walked over and sat next to him, waiting for him to acknowledge her presence before talking.

"Do you need something?" he said playfully.

She had sat there staring for a good minute. "What have you been thinking about?" she asked, severe curiosity in her eyes.

He looked at her with a suspicious smile, then shook his head and laughed. "Something impossible and probably a waste of my thoughts," he answered.

But Sara knew what he was talking about. "You want to try and break her curse," she said, hoping her instincts were right.

He gave her a surprised look. "Yes," he said. "I mean, I would at least like to try."

"I want to help," Sara said excitedly. Duncan gave her a suspicious look. There was a motive behind her eyes that he couldn't put a finger on, but it didn't seem sincere.

"Why?" he asked.

"Because…" she hesitated, "she is our new friend and I wanna help her." Duncan accepted this.

"I don't even know where to start," he said, unsure if it was even a good idea. "It's true. You really can't break another person's curse. That's part of the 'curse' part; you're stuck with it forever."

Sara had done some thinking too, and she had her own idea. "Maybe the Naturals lied to Astrid," she said. "Maybe there is a way, they just don't like to take the risk of interfering with someone else's curse."

Duncan had considered that while he was lost in thought, but he was surprised Sara had come up with the idea herself. It was definitely just a guess, but it wouldn't hurt to do some research and see if it was possible. And Duncan knew just where to go.

Chapter 20

A few hours later, Carter and Grayson woke up at the same time. Since Grayson was Carter's creator, they had a strong connection that allowed them to share some experiences, like feelings of fatigue and hunger.

In some ways, they had grown apart because of the situation with Sara choosing Grayson over Carter. But ever since Astrid had come into the picture, Carter had loosened up. His connection with Grayson had improved.

However, it was unbeknownst to them that Duncan and Sara had not yet gone to sleep.

When they came downstairs, Sara was sitting quietly next to Duncan while he read through his spell books. He didn't think the answer to breaking Astrid's curse would be in there, but he decided to give it a try before he left.

Grayson looked concerned. "Why did you not come to bed?" he asked, almost angry at himself for not staying awake till she came into the room.

"I'm not tired," she said, although it was a lie. She didn't need as much sleep as regular vampires because of her day-walking spell, but she did need it. But that day, she was too invested. "I stayed up with Duncan because he's leaving soon."

Both Grayson and Carter looked shocked. "Why are you leaving?" Carter asked. "This is probably the worst time! We have no idea where Mura is or when she will attack."

Duncan figured his friends would be concerned, but he also remembered that he'd never had time to tell the story of his mother and the Naturals' bookstore.

After he told them his story, they then understood why he might want to leave, but he decided to clarify anyways. "If I go live with my mother in the bookstore," he started, "not only will I learn better spells, become a stronger Natural, and be exposed to all kinds of different Naturals, I'll get to spend time with my mother. I can still keep you all safe, even from far away. And with my teleportation spells, I can be back here in an instant."

The true reason he was leaving was to use the help of his mother and the frequent guests of the store to find a way to break Astrid's curse. Honestly, he wasn't even sure he could live there, or if she would help him. But he was going to try.

Duncan ran upstairs to grab a few things while Grayson and Carter stood considering what he had just said. They were still worried about their friend leaving at such a dangerous time. But in minutes, he was back downstairs, carrying a small bag filled with his things. "Don't worry," he said, taking a few steps away from his friends. "I'll be back before you know it." And then he vanished before they could even try to stop him.

***

For a week, everyone stayed in their own homes. Outwardly, Carter and Astrid appeared to communicate minimally by texts, only enough to tell the other one they hadn't heard anything. But, in the daylight, while everyone else was busy, they would send messages of secrets, hopes, and dreams.

Duncan contacted Sara every day to tell her how his search was going. So far, he had found nothing. His mother swore there was no spell to break another's curse.

Although Carter, Sara, and Grayson didn't venture too far from home, after a week cooped up, Marcello and Astrid began looking for Mura again.

Marcello decided to rely on a few vampire friends he'd developed over the past two thousand years. None were as old as he was, but a few were over a thousand. He also contacted a few packs of werewolves he was friendly with, encouraging them to keep an eye out for the Willow family. He decided not to bother with his Natural friends. Most of them were very close, and he didn't want Jazel getting word that the Willow family was being looked for.

Astrid simply hunted, looking a few hundred miles away from the little town of Blessings. But she couldn't even pick up a scent that might lead her to the family. So after a few days, she came home. Her guard was still up when she arrived; it would be until Mura was killed. But it was nice to be home and have the feeling that Mura and her family might have moved away for good, possibly deciding to leave them alone.

When she got back to her house, the sun was going down. Marcello was still gone. He wanted to ask all his trusted friends to help, which meant even leaving the country to speak with a few. Although he could call them, supernatural were sometimes a little old-fashioned; they liked face-to-face communication, especially if it was important. She knew he'd probably be gone for a few more days. She worried about him, but she knew he could take care of himself.

It had been about two weeks since Duncan went to see his mother. Astrid sat on her balcony, twirling a glass of wine as she watched the sun come up. Her awake time had been shifted, so now mornings where her afternoons.

She couldn't help but think about Carter. Something about him made her feel safe, happy, and beautiful. She looked at her phone, staring at his number, thinking about what she wanted to do next. She stared so long, the sun finally appeared over the horizon. She had been so stressed for the past couple of weeks that she just wanted to relax. Maybe Mura was gone for good. She started to type, finished her text, and pushed the send button as she closed her phone and took a sip of wine. She wasn't sure what would happen next.

She had invited him over. Her words exactly where: *You should come over for a quick bite to eat.* No smiley face or anything else. She looked down at herself. Honestly, she was a mess. She sat there with her long hair down. She wore a thin white tank top that showed through to her blood-red bra. Her legs were bare except for a very short pair of cotton shorts; it was an outfit she'd never wear in public.

In the short time she'd been home, she'd painted the tips of her nails a dark red color. She looked at herself as she imagined him coming over to her house; she wasn't really dressed for company. *Except for maybe a certain kind of company.*

She lay on her fold-out porch chair, wondering if he would text her back. However, after a few minutes and multiple sips of wine, she put her phone down. *Maybe another day*, she thought, rolling over to her side.

But then, she heard quick feet racing toward her house. She sat up fast, looking to see who was coming. To her surprise, it was Carter, glowing in the cool morning air.

She walked over to the edge of the balcony, giving him a flirtatious smile. "You didn't text me back," she said from the balcony edge. Seeing his face made her fight not to grin giddily from ear to ear. She was happy to see him. She realized now how much she had missed his company the past couple of weeks.

"I thought I'd surprise you," he said. "I feel like I haven't seen you in months."

His remark made Astrid feel light. She liked Carter, and she liked his surprise.

"You should come up," she said, letting her smile show through.

In one quick jump, Carter was standing next to Astrid, only inches away from her body. The closeness surprised her, making her want to take a step back. But she felt a strange pull between them that kept her close.

Without asking, he closed the small gap between them even more, standing only a short distance from her body. Her skin began to tingle all over. Although she had experienced some lifetimes of being promiscuous, she hadn't been so close to anyone in a long time. It made it hard to breathe. She almost felt dizzy from excitement. The feelings rushing through her body almost made her scared. She couldn't remember a time she had ever felt that way. She felt like she was losing control of her body. It was terrifying and exciting all at the same time.

"Have I ever told you your smell is intoxicating?" she asked, her voice breathy and quiet, her eyes moving quickly, searching for the perfect place to look. But every place she glanced at on him was perfect and made her nervous.

"That's funny," he whispered back, his lips moving very slowly closer to her. "I was going to tell you the same thing."

Her knees almost gave out when he kissed her, and she fought hard not to let out a pleasurable sound when their lips touched. Endorphins exploded through her body, every inch feeling electric. He touched his hand softly to her back as they kissed, and she reached her hand to the back of his neck, ready to hold tight if he pulled away. She didn't want the kiss to end.

Suddenly, she was off the ground, held tightly in his arms. She knew she had to be under some kind of spell if she let that happen. She should have seen that coming. But she liked the spell. It made her feel loved and wanted, a feeling she rarely experienced.

He made his way inside her house, still holding her securely, their lips still locked. Both doors were open, and he entered the wrong room, which made Astrid laugh. She attempted to leap out of his arms and lead him into her room, but as she struggled, he let out a faint growl under his breath and tightened his grip. He looked deep into her eyes, assessing her reaction.

Although it took her back, she laced her fingers into his hair, giving a gentle pull and placing her lips back onto his.

Carter made his way into Astrid's room, laying her gently on the bed. He began to rub his hands all over her body, feeling every soft curve. His pressure began to increase as his instincts kicked in. He began to feel wild, and without meaning to, his fangs appeared.

It caught him off guard, although Astrid wasn't surprised. He stopped for a minute, starting to create space between himself and her, but her hand pressed tightly on his lower back.

"What are you doing?" she asked, wondering why he was moving away.

"I'm sorry," he said. "Sometimes they have a mind of their own." He moved his hand to cover his mouth, and she reacted quickly, grabbing his arm tightly, looking directly at his fangs.

She moved his arm back down to the bed, and he looked at her curiously. She took her well-groomed hand and placed her finger on her neck, scraping a small cut across her skin with her nail. Carter's eyes widened.

"I think they were just reading my mind," she whispered, waiting to see how he would respond.

In an instant, the wild hunger returned to his eyes. It was a look mixed with the desire for pleasure and the desire for blood. He looked intensely at her neck for a moment, taking in the sight and sweet smell of her blood. Then, he looked deep into her eyes. He could see what she wanted.

In one quick motion, he pressed his fangs deeply into her neck, feeling the sweet rush of her warm blood fill his mouth. She took a deep breath when he first bit her, as if it might have hurt. But then the venom from his fangs rushed through her body, and she was left with nothing but pleasure.

Chapter 21

For the next several weeks, while Marcello was gone, Carter and Astrid stayed together. Carter spent most of his time at Astrid's house, and they occasionally went out on the town. Carter learned the secret that Astrid's blood replenished itself almost immediately.

As a vampire hunter, it was interesting that Astrid also made the best vampire partner. She healed quickly, and, after being fed on, her blood levels were back to normal in minutes.

She taught him about stealing blood bags from donation centers so he and his friends could avoid feeding on humans. Although humans needed the blood from blood banks, it was better than attacking a human in the night to feed.

When Marcello finally returned, Carter and Astrid's time together didn't diminish. Instead, they shifted between his house and her house while Astrid tried hard to still spend time with Marcello. She had missed him and worried about him while he was gone. He, unfortunately, had been unsuccessful. Either no one wanted to talk about the Willow family or they just didn't know where they were. They had no leads on their location, and it was stressful.

Duncan continued searching for a way to break Astrid's curse. He read every spell book he could get his hands on, even searching through histories and potions books, trying to find even a mention of breaking a curse. His mother watched him closely.

He would stay up late into the night and wake up early in the morning. He got lost in the books, sometimes forgetting to eat and sleep. The good thing was he was learning a lot, more than most Naturals. The bad part was that intensely searching was physically hurting his body. His mother was worried.

Grayson and Sara weren't as relaxed as Carter and Astrid were. They were still concerned about Mura and worried that she would attack. But in Astrid's mind, there wasn't much they could do but wait and see if one of Marcello's friends got a lead on the Willow family's location.

Sara became tense anytime Carter and Astrid came around. Although she was with Grayson, she couldn't deny she had feelings still for Carter. Seeing him with Astrid didn't help calm her vampire emotions. All she wanted was good news from Duncan that he had found a way to break her curse. Then, she could go through with her secret plan.

Astrid noticed Sara's tension and one day, she brought it up with Carter. "I feel like your friends don't like me," she started, "or at least don't like us together."

He sighed at the unasked question. It was something he didn't like talking about. "It's just Sara," he said. "She's… jealous, I guess."

"But she's with Grayson," Astrid said.

"I know," he agreed, "but ever since she became a vampire, she's been more… emotional. She seems a bit more confused about who she wants to be with."

Astrid hesitated. "Who do you want to be with?" she asked.

Carter looked confused and a little hurt. "I don't want to be with Sara," he insisted. "I've already been down that road with her, and I'm done with it. She can be jealous all she wants."

Astrid smiled and gave him a sweet kiss. The hurt in his eyes disappeared, and he smiled back at her.

***

Things continued the same way for several more weeks. Astrid and Carter spent this time in his sheets, talking and loving. Sara and Grayson kept their distance while Marcello constantly checked on Duncan at the Natural's library. Then, two weeks before Astrid's birthday, her positive attitude disappeared. She became filled with anxiety, anger, and frustration. She quickly distanced herself from everyone, which Carter noticed very soon after it happened.

Astrid had gone home that night to spend time with Marcello. Carter had sent a few texts just asking how she was doing. Although she never responded, Carter didn't think anything of it. He thought she was probably just having fun with Marcello.

But the next day, when he called in the morning, she didn't answer. Now he was worried, but he waited a while before going over. He called a few more times, and by nighttime, he was rushing over to her house.

***

Duncan's mother had been watching him carefully for the several weeks he stayed with her at the store. He had been killing himself looking for a way to break Astrid's curse, and one day, his mother finally decided to tell him a secret.

"Duncan," she started, "interfering with someone else's curse is a dark matter. To do it, you have to use dangerous magic, one only a few Naturals approve of using."

He wasn't sure yet what she meant, but he listened closely. He knew she had probably been lying when she told him it was impossible to break another Natural's curse. That was one reason he'd been searching so hard. He wanted her to see how serious he was about helping his friend. And it looked like all the hard work had paid off.

"What do I do?" he asked, ready for anything.

Paige stood up and led her son into the basement of the building. The door was locked and bound tight, so he had never been down there. The basement was where the spell books that contained dark magic were kept.

"These spells are called Shadows," she said, picking up a small book left resting on a table. It was covered with a thick layer of dust.

People must very rarely come down here, Duncan thought.

"Shadows are no stronger than regular magic, but they do things that are against nature. These spells can restore life, take life, and cause great pain. But they can also be of use to you."

She walked over to a dark part of the room, and without searching, picked up the exact book she needed from the shelf. It was a dark purple, although when she opened it, it changed to black.

"When I inherited this store from the last Natural," she began, "the knowledge and spells from every book were given to me. I know where every spell book is and every single spell inside. This is the book where you will find the solution to your friend's curse. But I warn you, Duncan. Shadows almost have a life and spirit to themselves. If you use them too much, sometimes even once, they can consume your body, making you a Natural of the Shadows. For every Natural, it's different. Some use these Shadows occasionally and are still free to use their good magic. Others try a Shadow once and are changed forever."

He thought about the words she said. Was he really willing to risk that much for his friend? But he felt strong.

After the two months he spent there, he felt like he could handle anything. One Shadow in his entire life would probably not hurt him. At least, he hoped it wouldn't.

He reached his hand out to his mother, ready to take the book from her. "I'm willing to take the risk," he said.

She looked at him worriedly. "Take this book, find the spell you're looking for, and then go help your friend. But don't take this book with you. It cannot leave this room. This basement is bound to keep the Shadows in. Only remember the words of the spell you wish to take with you. Don't let the other one's escape into your mind."

With those words, she handed him the book. And he sat reading until he found what he was looking for: a spell to break Astrid's curse.

***

The lights were on when Carter made it to Astrid's house. Since the sun was down, he knew Marcello was awake. He tapped lightly on the door. In an instant, Marcello had opened it, stepped outside, and closed the door behind him, standing next to Carter. "We need to talk," Marcello said, very softly but with urgency.

They sat on the stairs, and Marcello looked very sad. "What's wrong?" Carter asked, worried something had happened to Astrid.

"Astrid has…" he paused, trying to find the words to say. Then he sighed. "Astrid has shut down. That's the best way to put it. It's happened before, but I've never seen it this bad."

"What do you mean she's shut down?" Carter asked, confused.

"In less than two weeks," Marcello started, "Astrid's going to die. There's nothing we can do about it. And when she passes, you and your friends won't remember who she is. I think last night it finally hit her that the relationship between you and your friends that she's developed will be gone shortly. So she shut down. She's still unresponsive. Carter, she's given up. Like I said, it's happened before, but never this bad."

Carter looked down. He didn't know what to do. "Where is she?" he asked, thinking maybe he could try to talk her out of it—get her to enjoy these last couple weeks with him.

"She's in her room," Marcello said. "However, you can't go in there."

Carter looked in disbelief. "Why not?" he asked.

"Well, the door is locked, and if you try to break it down, she'll attack you," Marcello said, almost with a smile on his face as he awkwardly rubs his hands through his hair. He had been dealing with it all day, and by that point, smiling was all he could do not to get mad. "And if you talk too much, she'll attack you, and if you do make it in the room, she'll attack you. She's very persistent. I wouldn't go in there, Carter. At this moment, she has no reason not to just kill you. I'm only still alive because I'm the only one who will remember her."

Then, they heard running toward the house, and, to their surprise, Sara appeared in front of them. "Where's Astrid?" she asked Marcello with a wicked smile on her face. She ignored Carter so her mood wouldn't drop. "I have some good news to tell her."

"Uh," Marcello said, still wondering why Sara was there. "She's not really seeing anyone today… or for the next two weeks. I was just telling Carter I wouldn't go in there."

Sara looked confused, but she shook her head and burst into the house anyways. "Oh, fuck," Marcello said, running inside behind her.

"Astrid, I need to talk to you," Sara called from outside Astrid's room. "I have some really good news." By then, Marcello and Carter were near Sara. Marcello stood close, in case the door flung open and Astrid appeared, ready to kill. They only heard silence from behind the door, not even the slightest sound of movement. "Oh, please don't make me tell you through the door. It's too good for that."

They waited for a moment, but there was still no sound. Marcello was right. Astrid had completely given up. However, Sara hadn't.

"Listen, I need to tell you something," Sara started. "For the past two months, Duncan has been living with his mother at the spell bookstore."

Before she could continue, Astrid swung open the door, ready to attack. Marcello jumped quickly in front of Sara, anticipating Astrid would do this. Carter saw Astrid and desperately wanted to talk to her but she implies stared at Marcello.

"Please, Astrid, just let her talk," Marcello pleaded. Astrid's face calmed, and she rolled her eyes, crossing her arms. Sara continued, somehow unaffected by Astrid's negative demeanor.

"I know where he has been," Astrid said in a condescending tone.

"Anyway," Sara started again, "he's been doing some research while he was there, and he thinks he may have found a way to break your curse!"

Everyone stood silent, taking in the news. Astrid looked suspiciously at Sara. "How?" she asked.

Sara laughed. "How should I know? I'm not a Natural. But he's coming back tonight to talk to us about it. He should be here soon. You have to come over now."

Astrid stared at Sara for a moment. She was trying to decide if she wanted to start caring again or not. She had already shut down, and it was tough to get her out of it. But she glanced over at Carter who stood desperately looking at her. She didn't want him to forget her because she would never forget him.

She looked at all three vampires standing before her. They all look so hopeful and full of life. They were all excited by the news. No one knew if it would work, but at least they had a chance to break Astrid's curse. So she went into her room, grabbed her jacket, and said with only a little enthusiasm, "What are we waiting for, then?"

Chapter 22

When they arrived at the other house, Astrid's mood began improving as they waited for Duncan to arrive. She was skeptical that any of it was going to work, but it felt good to have friends who were trying to help.

Carter had been hesitant as they ran over to his house, but he sat next to Astrid, holding her hand. She smiled at his presence. *Maybe things will be okay*, she hoped to herself.

Duncan suddenly appeared, carrying nothing in his hands. Astrid expected to see some kind of spell book or something tagging along with him. All he carried was hope on his face with a fraction of worry in his eyes.

"Good, you're all here," he said when he saw everyone gathered in the living room. "I'm guessing Sara already told you why."

"I did," she said proudly, although her part in helping Astrid had been very small so far. Duncan was the one who'd done all the work.

He began by explaining some things his mother had told him about Shadows and the basement filled with those dark spells. He left out the part about Shadows being dangerous to use. He didn't want to worry his friends. But the mentioning of dark magic made them worried already.

"Are you sure you should be messing with those types of spells?" Grayson asked, not nearly as committed to helping Astrid as everyone else was.

"Yes," Duncan answered confidently. "It's not the spell itself that I'm worried about; it's the timing of when it must be done. I have to use this spell at the most critical time possible in the cycle of Astrid's curse to ensure that it works."

"Which means you have to wait till the second I turn twenty-five to use the spell," Astrid said, "risking missing the opportunity to use it."

"Yes," he answered, this time with less enthusiasm. "And there's one more thing." Everyone looked at him anxiously, although Astrid was pretty sure she knew what the condition was. "Since you went from being a vampire to a vampire hunter, you can't go back to being a human. Someone has to turn you while the spell is happening. Or you'll just die forever."

This strange catch to the spell intrigued Astrid. She had assumed she would just have to become a vampire. But she had never been faced with such different options before. The first time she turned, she never had a choice. She died in Marcello's arms, and he turned her to keep her alive. Then she was cursed, and she definitely had no say in that.

But at that point, she was faced with two very different options: continue to live forever as a vampire or finally put an end to it all and let her spirit finally rest for good. It wasn't going to be an easy choice.

"So, I can either choose to live forever or finally die forever," she said to herself, although everyone was listening.

"Well, the choice is obvious," Carter said, hoping Astrid would agree. Of course she would become a vampire.

"I'll have to think about it," Astrid said, rushing out the door, leaving everyone in a state of shock.

***

Marcello followed Astrid home and sent a message out to everyone a few hours later that Astrid wanted to be left alone for a few days. Duncan was somewhat offended by her actions. He had worked so hard and spent so much time trying to help her, and she didn't even thank him.

Carter was hurt because Astrid had left without saying goodbye, and she didn't want him there while she made her decision. They had grown very close, and he began to wonder how much she really cared for him. He tried to think of her and the decision she had to make, but all he couldn't think about was that he may have found the person he wanted to spend the rest of his long life with. And he wanted her to want him. And right now, she just wanted to be alone.

Duncan stayed in town for a few days, spending some quality time with his friends. He had not seen or even really spoken to them in two months, and he missed them. He decided he would probably come back to the house to stay, but he needed to return to the spell bookstore to get his things and say goodbye to his mom.

But to Duncan's surprise, when he arrived one evening, his mother wasn't there. It was strange because he didn't think she could leave and that she was bound to the store, but she never answered the door, and he couldn't find her when he went inside.

After searching for a few minutes for his mother, he started to feel strange; there was a dark energy filling up the building. His instinct was to run, but he had to find his mom. He didn't understand why she wasn't there. Then he heard a strange voice call his name from behind, and when he turned around, he saw his mother lying motionless on the ground, her eyes opened wide. But it wasn't her who called his name.

He was about to rush toward her when he saw the origin of the voice: it was Jazel. She was close, standing directly over his mother, that same cold look on her face.

"Don't worry," she said, her eyes looking straight into Duncan with her cold, raspy voice. "She's not dead, just sleeping for a while. You can't kill the guardians, but you can use some spells on them."

Rage filled Duncan's body. He wanted to attack and kill Jazel. But he wasn't sure if he could win. "What do you want?" he yelled, not looking away from her monstrous eyes.

"Nothing anymore," she answered, a secret tucked away deep behind her eyes. "She already told me what I wanted to know. I'll be seeing you soon, little Natural." She turned, but before she vanished, she added, "Oh, and Mura says hello." And then she was gone.

Duncan hurried over to his mother, who suddenly took a deep, painful breath, slowly moving her limbs and blinking her eyes. He held her hand as the spell began to wear off, and the life returned to her. She sat up, confused, clenching her still-aching chest. Duncan said a quick healing spell, hoping to speed up the recovery process.

"Are you okay?" Duncan asked as soon as he finished the spell. Her breathing returned to normal, and she let go of her chest, letting out a big sigh of relief as she began to recover.

"I think so," she said, smiling at her son.

"What happened?" he asked, helping his mother to her feet.

Paige stood for a minute, shaking her head, saying, "She… she tapped into my memories. She knows about you looking for a Shadow and finding one to break your friend's curse. Duncan, you are in danger. That woman is a Natural of the Shadows."

That's when it hit Duncan: if he used the Shadow spell he had found to save Astrid, he could turn into a Natural like Jazel. He shivered at the thought. *Would that make me evil, too?*

She looked sadly at her son. "I'm sorry, Duncan. I think you need to go back to your friends," she said, looking concerned.

Duncan didn't look convinced he should leave. His mother had just been attacked. He didn't want to leave her alone.

"I'll be fine," she reassured him, sensing his resistance.

He gave her a hug and quickly vanished, appearing at his house with his friends. "We need to go talk to Astrid," he said.

"But she didn't want to see us for a few days," Carter said with a hint of sarcasm, still hurt from her distancing herself from him.

"I think she's in danger," Duncan warned. Without hesitation, the group got up and made their way over to Astrid's house.

They knocked on the door when they arrived, waiting for an answer, but no one came. The three vampires were the first to show concern; they smelled fresh blood inside the house. Carter pushed the door open and rushed inside. Carter made his way upstairs toward the smell of Astrid's blood.

He saw red footprints stained in the carpet upstairs. He rushed into Astrid's room only to find a cold puddle of blood seeping into the floor. Astrid wasn't there, but Marcello was. He was desperate. It was daytime and he couldn't leave the upstairs area or he would die. But Astrid had been taken, but it was a struggle.

Carter continued to search, hoping to find her somewhere, maybe conscious but at least alive. However, his search came up with nothing.

Carter spoke. "Where's Astrid?" he asked, angry Marcello had failed to keep her safe.

But the one word Marcello spoke was enough to caused him alarm. "Mura," he said, still looking at the pool of blood in Astrid's room. She must have been ambushed.

Carter screamed with anger. He wanted Mura dead, and he wanted her dead that instant. He was tired of her games. He placed himself in front of Marcello, close to his face. "Where did they take her?" he asked, treating Marcello like some kind of enemy.

He was somewhat weak from needing sleep, but not weak enough to not get mad. "How would I know? You think I just *let* them take her?"

Carter stood back, still filled with rage. "How are we supposed to find her?" he asked.

Marcello sat silent and sad. He didn't know the answer to that question. Carter walked away while everyone watched as he tried to contain his frustration. Grayson, Sara and Duncan came rushing up the stairs. Carter looked at his friends, who were looking at the blood stained carpet. "They have her," Carter uttered.

"That's why I wanted us to rush over here," Duncan said, frustrated he had missed his chance to save Astrid. "My mother was attacked by Jazel and unwillingly showed her everything about Astrid. I was hoping we would get here before they came, but we were too late."

Everyone stood quiet for a while, taking in the news and the events that had just unfolded. But Duncan's thoughts were more conflicted than the rest.

While he was reading the spell book, his mother told him not to remember any of the other spells except the one he needed. However, every spell he read trying to find the right one stuck in his mind. So he knew how to find Mura and how to kill Jazel. But he would have to use Shadows, which his mother warned him only to do once to save Astrid.

"Tomorrow night at midnight, it will be Astrid's birthday," Marcello said. Marcello wasn't worried about Astrid being locked up with the Willow family. If they killed her, she would simply be reborn, and he would meet up with her again in sixteen years. But he would regret how close they were to breaking her curse. He was tired of the cycles. He wanted Astrid to be free.

"I think I can find Astrid," Duncan admitted. "I recently found some very… powerful spells while staying with my mom. I think I can use one to find her." He paused for a moment. "And I think I can kill Jazel as well."

Everyone looked surprised but hopeful. "Why didn't you say something before?" Carter asked.

"It just took me a while to remember the spells," he lied. "I wasn't a hundred percent sure they would work, but I think they will." Truly, he was worried about the ramifications of using the Shadows. But he couldn't get the spells out of his mind until he used them. "Unfortunately, some spells require the moon, while some require the sun. The first spell I can use because the sun is up."

Marcello frowned at that idea. Not only would he not be able to help, but it would also mean they would have less time to get Astrid, cutting close to the specific time Duncan would need to break her curse. Duncan noticed Marcello's grim look.

"Give me ten minutes," Duncan said as he teleported to an unknown location. Ten minutes later, after a few awkward minutes, Duncan reappeared in the room. "Here," Duncan said, handing a vile to Marcello. "I made you a potion so you can walk in the day. We'll definitely need your help."

Marcello was stopped short by that idea. He hadn't seen the sun in two thousand years. He wasn't even sure if he wanted to walk in the light again. But then, he thought about Astrid. He didn't want her to die alone, surrounded by people who hated her. He wanted to save her and break her curse.

"It would be an honor," Marcello said as he reached for the vile and was lost in the thoughts of walking in the sun again.

Duncan explained his plan. Once they found the Willow family, he would teleport everyone but himself to Astrid's location. Then he would send himself to where Jazel was. With the noon sun, he would have one chance to kill her. Unfortunately, Duncan's mind was filled with worry and fear. He didn't know what a Shadow spells would do to him, especially using three, but his thoughts gave him no hope that it would be good.

Grayson was the one to speak up. "I don't like that plan."

"Why not?" Duncan asked.

"Because," Carter chimed in, "you will be alone with Jazel. Let one of us help you. We can distract her."

Duncan considered this. A distraction would help, but that would put his friends lives in danger. But then Grayson insisted, "I will go with you to see Jazel," Grayson stated. "Everyone else can go to where Astrid is."

Sara frowned, but Grayson placed his hand on her shoulder. "We can do this," Grayson said to her. She didn't smile, but she did nod her head. She had her own plan for when Astrid was no longer cursed, but she kept that to herself.

Marcello looked suspiciously at the magical vile he held in his hand. It was a creamy orange color and as he sniffed it, it smelled like sweat. Carter tapped his shoulder, "Just one small drop on the tongue."

Marcello smiled, took one last look at the bottle, and placed a small drop on his tongue, He wasn't sure what to expect. He stood for a moment, his senses heightened. Then he took a few cautious steps out of Astrid's room and down the stairs.

The first bit if light touch his toes. He paused as he let the warmth fill his bare feet. He waited to see if his skin would begin to burn, but it didn't. He smiled, almost cried, but before he could continue to gently step into the sun, the three vampires and Duncan came rushing down the stairs, pushing him into the light. He held up his hands in defense, but still, nothing happened.

"Come on," Carter said emphatically. "We have to save Astrid. No times for games."

Duncan was worried as he made his way out into the sun. They had a plan, but it had been foiled before. He also didn't know what was to become of him after today when he used the Shadows. But he knew he had to be strong. His friends were counting on him. Astrid was counting on him the most—and he wasn't about to let her down.

Chapter 23

Duncan went about rehearsing in his mind what he needed to do. First, find the location of Astrid, Mura, and Jazel. Next, send his friends to Astrid. Then, send himself and Grayson to the location of Jazel. Finally, render Jazel powerless and kill her.

His hope was that he would catch everyone off guard. He especially hoped Jazel would be confused if he used a Shadow instead of a regular spell, allowing him to defeat her.

As the sun came closer to noon, everyone gathered outside together, waiting for Duncan to begin the process. He pulled out a blank piece of paper and began using his first Shadow to try and locate his three targets. It wasn't the same spell his mother had used. Unfortunately, that spell wasn't strong enough to get past Jazel's powers and locate everyone. But his Shadow would do the trick.

Duncan focused hard, and after a few seconds, a map appeared on the page, along with three small symbols. Unfortunately, he had not calculated for a flaw in his plan. Although he knew the color for Astrid and vampires, he didn't know the color for Naturals. And, although Mura was a type of vampire, apparently, Energies didn't show up as black. Instead, he stood looking at a purple dot, a green dot, and a white dot. He had no idea what the green and purple dots represented.

But as he looked at the map, the green indicator disappeared. He remembered his mother saying the maps couldn't always keep up because of how fast vampires could move. So, he decided to assume the green dot was Mura. That was a good thing because, at first, Mura was close to Astrid. But he hoped she'd moved away from her. And Jazel was nowhere near Astrid, although they were in the same house.

"What is that?" Carter asked after a few minutes of waiting. He had become impatient with Duncan's silence. "It looks like the blueprint of a house."

"It's a map showing the location of Mura, Jazel, and Astrid," he answered. "The map itself is actually more of a floor plan. It is showing the setup of the house where they all are."

"Are they close?" Grayson asked, everyone getting anxious to begin the rescue mission.

"No," Duncan admitted. "They're actually very far away, in Maine. But I can transport you there quickly. Are you guys ready for this?"

They examined the floor plan carefully, planning their escape route for when they had obtained Astrid. Marcello suggested a café he had been to before and for them to meet there once they had escaped the house. They all agreed, and Duncan gathered everyone together to begin his spell.

"Wait," Marcello said, rushing inside the house and coming out with a small bag. "I almost forgot." He handed everyone two medium-sized wooden stakes and even made sure Duncan took two, just in case. "It's always good to have a quick way to kill a vampire, or at least slow them down."

Duncan smiled. He didn't think he would need it, but it made him feel a little safer to have a backup plan. He began the transportation spell, and, after everyone gave each other one last look, they vanished from the house, planning to reappear near Astrid. As soon as they were gone, Duncan looked at

Grayson, gathered his strength again and sent them to what he thought would be the location of Jazel.

As his eyes refocused on his new location, to Duncan's horror, he wasn't where he wanted to be. Standing in front of him wasn't Jazel, but it was Mura. Apparently, the green dot was Jazel. He had guessed wrong. However, in her eyes, he could see surprise.

Grayson responded quickly to the new plan and attacked Mura, stake ready in hand. Mura didn't look scared, she simply moved out of the way and sent Grayson flying behind her. But he figured he couldn't kill her, he was just good distraction while Duncan gathered himself.

Without thinking, Duncan instantly used a spell to render her unconscious. He was worried it wouldn't work, but to his surprise again, it did. Her eyes rolled back, and she fell to the ground hard. He looked at her cautiously and with disbelief. But her stillness reassured Duncan that his spell had worked. He really wasn't sure what to do next.

However, Grayson once again was quick thinking and grabbed a tight hold on one his stakes and rushed over to Mura to kill her while she was unconscious.

Duncan quickly sensed a powerful presence behind him. When he turned, he saw Jazel standing motionless, anger flowing behind her cold, dark eyes.

That was his only chance left to attack. He quickly gathered up his strength, sending a lightning pulse of magic toward Jazel, stunning her, but only for a few moments. Duncan took that time to reconjure his strength, this time focusing hard on the energy of the sun and on the dark Shadow he remembered from the book he read.

He spoke the short words as quickly as he could, but Jazel gained her strength too quickly, and they attacked at the same time. It was like when two gunmen both shoot at each other simultaneously; they both end up getting shot. They just both hoped the other took the more fatal injury.

In this case, both Jazel and Duncan were struck by each other's magic. Duncan hit the floor quickly, flooded with an uncontrollable pain much like the one he felt when he helped Astrid a few months prior. He held tightly to his stomach, curled up into a ball on the floor. He couldn't even look to see whether his spell had worked against Jazel.

He imagined her standing there, watching him wither away from the pain. He tried to say another spell, one to heal himself, but the magic got caught in his throat, and instead, he continued to writhe.

He took long, sharp breaths, feeling like poison was rushing through his body. He was sure he would die. But after a few moments, the pain began to subside. His hands unclenched, his breath slowed, and his eyes opened. His body was sore, but he could think and move without any real issues.

He got up slowly, not wanting to see the cold eyes of Jazel staring at his anguish. But he didn't see her eyes. Instead, he saw her on the ground, still and quiet. He could neither hear her nor see any sign she was breathing.

He stood up, feeling less pain by the second, and walked over cautiously to her body on the ground. He realized he'd killed her. Jazel had attacked with a spell to cause Duncan severe pain, but to her surprise, he had attacked with a spell to end her life. Normally, there was a process that must be completed to fully kill a Natural. But Duncan knew that spell, the Shadow, had done the trick and killed her for good.

As he stared at her lifeless corpse on the ground, he felt a strange feeling flowing through him. An unusual magic began to fill his body. It felt different—stronger, but darker.

He began to worry as the dark magic filled his body. His eyes and skin felt funny.

Grayson stopped his movement toward Mura and looked at Duncan. Grayson looked at his friend and whispered, "Duncan?" in a sad, confused tone.

Duncan turned around and noticed a mirror mounted on the wall behind him. He rushed over and was greeted by a fearful stranger in the reflection. His eyes were pure black, and his skin glowed a blazing white. He began to panic. His heart raced, and all he could think to do was run. And so he did.

Duncan vanished from the house just as some vampire members of the Willow family came bursting into the room after hearing all the sounds from inside. He left Mura unconscious on the ground, but sent a lightning bolt of power to Grayson, sending him to Astrid's location. It was the only thing he could think to do to save Grayson.

Duncan knew the spell on Mura would wear off soon, but right then, he didn't care. He was too scared of himself to worry about anyone else. He disappeared into the shadows of the forest around the house, hoping the strange change would be gone soon.

***

The others were also experiencing some unusual setbacks to the plan. Although they had made it to Astrid's location, they didn't all make it in the same room, which ended up being a good thing.

Astrid was locked in a vampire-tight cellar that the team was having difficulty opening. But when they got there, Carter and Marcello were all on the outside of the cell, while Sara was stuck inside with Astrid. And Astrid wasn't looking too good.

When they had first arrived, Sara found Astrid lying face down on the ground, her arms and legs going every which way. From the marks on the floor, it was clear Astrid had been dragged to her current location. She rushed to Astrid's side, picking her face up and brushing the blood and dirt off of her.

Her eyes were barely open, and Sara couldn't get any response from her. Her breathing was slow and shallow, and she hoped maybe it was just because this curse cycle was about to end.

"No," said Marcello. "The curse will not affect her until right after midnight. This was something else. I think it was the work of Mura."

No one looked convinced. "How could Mura do this?" Sara asked, looking at her weakened friend.

"Mura is an Energy," Marcello reminded the vampires. "She feeds on strength and life. And that's one thing Astrid is lacking right now."

Everyone looked closely at Astrid. They had never seen the workings of an Energy vampire before—and they hoped they never would again.

Marcello went and barricaded up the entranceway into the room and stood watch while Carter tried to find a way to open the cell. Although Carter was strong, that door was made to be even-older-vampire proof. His strength was no match for it.

"Maybe we could blow it up," Carter suggested.

Marcello gave him a confused looked. "Did you happen to bring any explosives with you?" he asked sarcastically.

Carter rolled his eyes and continued to think of a way to open the door. The way it was set up, it almost appeared it was meant to be opened from the inside. There was no handle or lock on the outside that they could see.

"Maybe if we all try to push at the same time, it will open?" Carter suggested.

Marcello looked suspiciously at the door. He wasn't able to get it himself, but maybe if they all tried.

"There's a bit of the door on the inside sticking out that I can pull," Sara said as she made her way over to the tightly locked door.

At the same time, both male vampires pushed as hard as they could to try and open the locked door, while Sara pulled with all her strength. But just as they felt the door begin to budge and their hopes rise, they heard footsteps coming toward them. And it was a lot of footsteps. But to their surprise, Grayson appear, also outside of the cell.

"I don't think this is a good sign," Carter said as he noticed Grayson.

"It's not," Grayson said plainly.

They stopped quickly, staring at each other, each one hoping the other had a good idea. "We have to get out of here," Marcello said, looking over desperately at Astrid motionless on the floor.

"But what about them?" Grayson said, looking at Sara standing locked behind the cold door. They could hear the hinges breaking loose on the entranceway door. They were almost out of time.

"We can come back for them," Marcello said. "It would be stupid for us all to get caught." And with that, Marcello ran across the room, ripped off the steel bars covering a window, and bolted out, shattering the glass.

Carter gave one last glance to Astrid and followed Marcello. Grayson was the last to leave. He stood for a moment, locking his eyes tight with the woman he loved, trapped in a place of danger. "I'll come back for you," he promised.

She smiled a reassuring smile to show him that she would be okay. And just as the door to the room flew off its hinges, he was gone.

Chapter 24

When the Willow family vampires arrived at the cell containing Astrid, they were surprised to see she had gained a guest. Sara was scared, but she kept a stoic demeanor about her; she didn't want them to *know* she was scared. She let out a low growl as they laughed at her.

After getting over their confusion and shock, the vampires searched her to make sure she wasn't a threat to them.

Suddenly, Mura entered the room after awakening from her spell and hearing there was an unexpected guest on the property. Normally, she would have laughed with excitement when she realized who it was. But in that moment, she was furious. Jazel had been killed, and she wanted revenge more than ever on Sara, Astrid, and all their friends.

Although Sara's deeds had grown to be of lesser importance since Astrid killed far more of the Willow family than Sara's one kill, Mura was still in the mood for a little revenge. She hadn't forgotten about Sara. And Duncan was the next on her kill list.

Mura left Sara in the same cell as Astrid. She knew Sara was young and weak, and Astrid was completely useless in her current state, she had made sure of that. She saw neither of them as a threat. A few vampires went over to the open window and spent a long time sealing it shut again.

When they all left the room, the lights were turned out. All that was left on was a small blue light in the corner of the cell. She guessed it was a light for a camera watching their every move.

Even though Sara could see in the dark, the silent and cold room was still eerie. The concrete floors and walls made no corner of the room comfortable. Sara stayed by Astrid, worried mostly about her curse taking effect after midnight.

With the vampires in the building on high alert, she couldn't imagine anyone being able to get in and save them before midnight. She wondered what would happen when Astrid disappeared and she forgot all about her. What strange reason would be created for her being locked in this room?

She sat silently next to her still friend and hoped all the others had made it out safely.

***

Carter, Grayson, and Marcello arrived at the rendezvous point but sat cautiously inside, keeping an eye out for any following vampires. They had hoped all the smells of the town they were in would throw off anyone following their trail. They waited silently for a few hours, hoping Duncan would return. But after a while, the sun started to fade and everyone began to give up hope.

"Where could he be?" Grayson asked to himself as he looked intently out the window. "We need him to get back in the building." Grayson had decided to keep Duncan's transformation to himself. He didn't want to worry anyone more than they already were.

The silence continued as they waited for their friend, but by the time darkness began to really set in, everyone decided it was time to take action.

"We can't wait around all night," Marcello started. "We will have to find a way into the building ourselves. The longer they're in there, the more danger they are in."

Suddenly, a strange note appeared in front of Grayson. "What is this?" he asked, cautiously touching the mysterious piece of paper. He opened it slowly then read the letter aloud. "All, Jazel is dead. I hope you made it out safely. Don't wait for me. I will meet you another time. I have something I have to do first. Duncan."

They weren't sure if they should believe the letter or not. It could have been sent by Jazel to encourage them to return to the manor and enter some sort of trap.

"Why would he not meet us?" Carter wondered. "I don't like this. Something seems fishy. What about breaking Astrid's curse?"

But Marcello wasn't interested in the letter and had given up hope on her curse being lifted. "We don't have time to worry about this note," Marcello said. "We can only hope Duncan is okay. Right now, we need to focus on saving Astrid and Sara."

Carter and Grayson were surprised at Marcello's lack of interest in the mysterious letter. But at least he was focused on saving the kidnapped girls.

"But what are we supposed to do?" Grayson asked. "The place is probably heavily guarded, and we aren't positive Jazel is dead. And after seeing what Mura can do, I definitely don't want to go one-on-one with her."

They sat for what felt like forever, bouncing ideas off each other, but by the time midnight started creeping close, Marcello had enough of the discussions. "I'm leaving," he said, standing up from the table where they had ordered food and drinks but had never eaten anything.

"How are you going to get in?" Carter asked.

"I'm just going to try," he said, walking out of the door while Carter and Grayson quickly followed. "I'm going to try and sneak in. Whether I get caught or not, who cares? I'm not going to sit around while Astrid dies. I can only hope Duncan is still planning on doing the spell at midnight. But I can't wait. I don't' know if Astrid is going to die forever, become a vampire, or disappear for 16 years. I can't wait to find out. I need to know. I have to be there if these are her last moments alive." And with that, Marcello stood and made his way to the new Willow Manor followed by Grayson and Carter.

When they arrived, they could sense the alertness and movement inside. There were vampires standing guard outside, and there were surely more doing the same inside. But Marcello had an idea. "I'm going to distract them," he said, getting ready to make his move.

Carter and Grayson gave him a look of disbelief.

"I think I can keep them occupied for a while. I want you to wait a few minutes and go in after me. Go through the same window we escaped from last time." And then he was gone.

Instantly, the guards noticed him, even with his super-fast movements. He was certainly good at getting everyone's attention. He was too quick for them to catch. All the vampires (except Mura) in this family were extremely young by vampire standards, so he was able to keep the occupied. He eventually busted through the front door, making his way inside. The guards outside were then called in, allowing the two vampires left behind to make their move. But as they reached the window that they had exited from early that day, they were met with despair; the window had been bolted shut with metal too strong for either of them to break.

They then heard the loud cry of a vampire inside and realized it was Marcello. They looked at each other with concern, and Carter pointed out, "This was a bad idea."

Suddenly, an energy filled the air as clouds quickly moved in and the wind began to pick. Carter and Grayson looked at each other, while Carter then glanced at his phone. "It's almost midnight," Carter said. They wondered what was going to happen to Astrid, although they would know soon if they were still going to remember her or not.

***

Duncan had been beside himself all day long. He was terrified of his own being. He couldn't bring himself to look in a mirror or even glance at his hands. The image he saw inside the manor haunted his vision and thoughts.

He had spent most of the day and evening curled under a small rock cave in the darkness, not even brave enough to open his eyes. He felt the air chill around him as the night came in. He finally risked a look into the darkness, still too scared to see himself.

It was at that moment he sent the message to his friends. He knew they would be worried, but he didn't want to let anyone see him. He felt like a monster; dark black eyes, paper-white skin. He couldn't tell, but at one point, he thought his teeth may have grown sharper. He looked like Jazel, and that made him hate himself.

As the darkness completely settled in, he finally emerged from his hiding space and made his way over to a bubbling river for a drink of water. The spells had left him tired and dehydrated.

As he looked in the water, the moon gave just enough light for him to see his reflection in the water. To his relief, his eyes were back to normal, and so was his skin color. And his teeth weren't as sharp as he thought they might be.

He stood looking at himself for a while, happy to be back to normal. But the reflection of the moon reminded him of something: Astrid. He wasn't sure if she was still in the manor or not, but as he looked at his phone for the time, he panicked. He might be too late. It was almost midnight. He didn't have time to transport himself to her. He needed to use the spell right then.

But he hesitated for a moment. It wasn't a normal spell he was using; it was a Shadow. The same type of spell that had deformed his image so badly before. He paused because he wasn't sure if using another Shadow would make that transformation permanent.

He looked at his phone: *12:00.* He had to decide immediately, and he did. He put down his phone, stood up, and began to recite the words of the Shadow spell he had learned only a few weeks ago. He realized Astrid would die if she didn't change into a vampire, but it was a risk he was pretty sure she would be willing to take.

***

After a long time of sitting in the strange blue light, Sara decided to turn it off. She walked over to the place where it was glowing. She found the small camera keeping an eye on them. It was set firmly in the wall, though the lens stuck out just enough for Sara to mess with it.

She found a small rock on the ground, and after a few tries, she finally jumped at the right height and smashed the small lens, leaving the rock behind in its place. She waited for someone to come in and yell at her or attack her for breaking the camera. But no one ever came. Unfortunately, the little light didn't go out. It was mounted too far inside the wall for Sara to get to, so she simply let herself feel reassured that no one was watching her anymore.

Astrid suddenly made a sound that sent Sara jumping into the air with fear. It was a loud, painful breath that sounded like her throat was almost closed. She continued to screech, reaching for her throat as if she couldn't breathe. Sara rushed over, trying to calm her down. After being so still all day, it was very alarming to have Astrid suddenly flailing around in pain.

The whites of Astrid's eyes began to turn red. Sara began to panic. She didn't know what to do for her friend, and it killed her to watch her suffer. Then she had a quick thought. *What time is it?* she wondered, remembering the curse would kill her at midnight. Unfortunately, there was no way to tell the time, but she asked, "Is this the curse?"

Astrid's eyes flashed toward Sara, and with a quick nod, she confirmed to Sara that it was the curse; in moments, she was going to die.

Sara sat there for a moment, holding Astrid's hand, trying to comfort her as much as she could. There was nothing she could do. Duncan wasn't there to break the curse. Astrid was just going to die.

In her panic, Sara did the only thing she could think to do to try and save her Astrid. She knew it wouldn't work, but she had to try anyway. She couldn't just sit and watch her die.

Sara's fangs quickly showed themselves, and in one swift bite of Astrid's neck, she drained as much blood as possible from her body. Then, before Astrid's eyes closed from death, Sara took a deep bite of her own wrist and dropped her fresh, warm blood in Astrid's mouth, hoping that just maybe a miracle would happen.

Astrid's eyes closed, her heart stopped, and her breathing vanished.

Chapter 25

Duncan fearfully looked at himself again in the river after performing the spell; he had once again changed into the terrifying creature from before. But this time, he didn't turn away. He stared at his reflection until, after a few minutes, it finally returned to normal.

He wondered if Jazel looked the way she did because he always saw her when she was performing a spell. He tried to imagine what she may have looked like in her normal form, but he couldn't imagine anything beautiful. He also wondered if the Shadow spell he used had broken Astrid's curse. He decided to go find out.

He used a locator spell to find his friends. He was interested to sense Sara and Astrid together, but Marcello, Grayson, and Carter weren't in the same spot. And Marcello was somewhere surrounded by the Willow family and Mura.

He decided to start where Carter and Grayson were waiting. He stood up, whispered his transportation spell to himself, and appeared next to his friends, sending them both back in shock.

"Where have you been?" Carter asked forcefully after recovering from the sudden appearance of Duncan.

"I'll explain later," Duncan responded. "What's going on?"

Carter quickly explained their earlier adventure inside the house, losing Sara behind the cell wall, and waiting for Duncan all day at the café. At that point, they were all crouched outside a boarded-up window, and Marcello was kidnapped inside. Carter and Grayson had been trying to come up with a plan.

"What are you doing out here?" Duncan asked. "How come you aren't inside?"

"The window is blocked!" Carter said and growl under his breath.

"You are helpless without me," Duncan teased, but only Grayson thought it was funny.

"I can kill Mura," Duncan said confidently. The Shadows had made him much stronger, though he was still concerned about what the permanent ramifications would be for using them too much. "I already killed Jazel, and Mura should be an easy target now."

They were surprised at how sure Duncan was of himself. But they weren't in a place to argue with him.

"So," Carter said, looking at Duncan, "what's the plan, then?"

The plan was for Duncan to transport Carter and Grayson inside the cell where Sara and Astrid were. He would transport himself to Mura since she was magic-free and vulnerable without Jazel. Finally, he would find Marcello, send them both into the cell, then transport them all out and home safely.

It seemed too easy, but it was a better option than anything Carter and Grayson had thought of, so they agreed to the plan. They realized then how much they relied on Duncan's magic and how annoying that was.

Instantly, they were inside the dark room, and Sara quickly wrapped her hands around Grayson, tears on her face. Carter made his way over to Astrid, anxious to see if she was okay. It was after midnight, but he still remembered her. He hoped that meant she was okay.

He looked cautiously at her cold, dead body on the ground. Sadness and rage filled him.

"I'm sorry," Sara said. "I tried to change her, but without Duncan, I think she just died. Maybe it takes a while to forget her."

Carter sat next to Astrid on the ground, holding her cold body the same way he had when he had found her lying unconscious, wounded, and in a pool of blood on his floor. He hoped that like last time, she would wake up. But the unknown was killing him inside.

Duncan, however, was not thinking at all about Astrid's current state. After he sent his friends inside, he transported himself into the same room as Mura. She looked at him vengefully as he appeared in the room. She wasn't surprised to see him. A handful of vampires were gathered with her in the room. It was strange to see her so guarded. At first, his friends had been fighting to protect themselves from her. But with Jazel gone, Mura was trying to protect herself from them. Duncan smiled at the thought of her fearing him.

He saw Marcello lying in the corner of the room on the floor. He was unconscious, and a stake rested in his abdomen.

The vampires in the room began to attack, but in an instant, Duncan had transformed again into the dark Shadow-wielding Natural he had become, and they all hit the floor, wailing equally in the same agonizing pain. But Mura didn't look scared. She just looked angrier.

Faster than his eyes could see, she appeared before him, her eyes shining with a strange blue glow. He began to feel weak. The white color drifted from his skin, returning to the dark olive-colored tint. He didn't understand what was happening.

Her eyes grew brighter as she took his energy. For a moment, he couldn't think straight. Then, he remembered Mura wasn't a normal vampire. He thought of how Carter had described Astrid drained of all her energy. And he knew he didn't want that to happen to him.

Duncan took a deep breath, centering his magic. If she wanted his energy, she could have it in the form of a spell. In one huge blast, he sent a binding spell toward Mura, knocking her backward and motionless. She looked angrily in Duncan's direction. He could see the spell wouldn't hold her for long. She was simply absorbing the energy from the magic surrounding her.

So Duncan did something he had never done before. He removed one of the stakes Marcello had given him earlier in the day, cursed it with a little extra magic, and sent the stake plunging straight into her heart.

Mura looked shocked. She stopped fighting the binding spell around her and fell to her knees. The stake lodged itself deep in her chest. Duncan had made it so it would never be able to be removed.

She fell to her side on the floor, a lightning-bright flash emitted from her body, and all that was left was the white ash of a dead vampire. Duncan stood still. He could sense another couple dozen or so in the large house. Some were headed for the room he was in.

He rushed over to Marcello, and he used a spell to transport them into the cell with Astrid and everyone else. They were all relieved to see both he and Marcello alive, and Grayson did the honors of removing Marcello's stake while he was still asleep. The pain, however, woke him up.

When he realized where he was, he crawled over to Astrid, who was still seemingly dead; he had a look of hope in his eyes, though, which made Carter wonder if maybe she was still alive.

They were finally all together, and Duncan could transport them all out before any of the other vampires came into the room. From upstairs, they heard the screams.

"Mura's dead," Duncan said, which explained the sounds.

Mura was the leader of their family, and she was gone. But as Duncan was about to send everyone away, Astrid woke up.

She shot up quickly from her cradled spot in Carter's arms. The surprise of her waking made everyone jump a little, although Marcello looked like he might cry. She looked around the room; fear and surprise filled her eyes.

Even Duncan then heard the sounds of feet rushing down the stairs. "We have to go," he said, getting ready to send everyone home.

"Where are Mura and Jazel?" Astrid asked, realizing there were other things that needed to be dealt with before she could take in what had happened to her.

"They're both dead," Duncan said, motioning everyone to join hands.

"But what about the rest of the family?" Astrid asked.

Marcello, who had also hesitated to join the group, knew what Astrid was thinking about.

"Who cares about them?" Duncan shouted. "We need to leave."

She nodded to Marcello as she walked over to the steel door, ripping it off the wall with all her might. Everyone stood in shock, but Marcello simply linked hands with Sara.

"You never kill one member of a vampire family," Astrid said. "You always kill them all." Then she vanished. But the sound of war followed her. All but Marcello stood in horror as Astrid made her way through the house, killing every vampire she saw.

Marcello changed his mind. He let go of Sara's hand and motioned everyone else to go on. But Duncan was in too much shock to send everyone away. "She's killing them all," he said in horror. "They haven't done anything!"

"They will," Marcello insisted. "Families are vengeful. Even if you kill their leader, the next oldest will take that spot. And they will all continue the revenge. You can never kill just one family member. Astrid is saving your lives. She's making sure no one from the Willow family will ever come after you again."

But their faces showed they still could not see why over so many vampires had to die.

"Just go home," Marcello said. And he also vanished into the darkness of Willow Manor to help Astrid do what had to be done.

***

Duncan, Sara, Grayson, and Carter all returned home in the middle of the night, exhausted. They couldn't decide how they felt about the vampire massacre that occurred at Willow Manor in Maine. But at the moment, they didn't care. They were so tired and so happy to be home. And they were all too curious about Astrid coming back to life.

"I turned her," Sara said as they began to discuss the events of the night. "She woke up in extreme pain, and she said it was the curse. So, I turned her. I wasn't sure what would happen, but I had to try."

Duncan almost laughed at how his spell had turned out. "I can't believe it all worked out," he said. "I remembered her curse right at midnight and used the spell to break it. I thought she would be dead, though. I didn't think anyone would have been turning her at the same time."

"I'm a little confused, though," Sara said, thinking about Astrid's change. "When I became a vampire, it was the most painful experience of my life. But that didn't seem to happen to Astrid."

Grayson was the one to answer her question. "Some vampires are lucky," he started, "and they don't wake until the most painful part of the process is complete. Most, however, aren't that lucky."

"Looks like Astrid was," Carter said, looking out the window. He was once again waiting anxiously to see if Astrid was okay. He didn't know if she would go there when she came home, but he hoped he could maybe smell her return and go check on her. Sara looked away in irritation, as if she were jealous of Astrid's easy transformation. She seemed to forget all the other things Astrid had been through.

Duncan began to stretch out his limbs. If anyone had been through a lot that night, it was him. He thought about explaining some of the things that had happened to him, but tiredness overcame him. He made his way upstairs to his room, giving his friends a grateful smile. "Let me know if Astrid comes over," he said. Then, he dragged himself the rest of the way to his room, falling asleep only seconds after lying down.

Sara and Grayson decided Duncan probably had the best idea. They said their goodnights to Carter and disappeared into their room upstairs. Carter, however, did not sleep. He sat up until dawn, waiting to see if he could sense Astrid returning home.

The light rising above the horizon sent shocks of worry through his mind. Astrid didn't yet have a potion to keep her safe in the daylight. After all, she had become a real vampire. He worried she may have not yet found shelter.

As the morning light fully set in, and noon was right around the corner, Carter lost all patience. He opened the door and ran quickly over to Astrid's, hoping to see signs that she had come home.

As he reached the door, he knew he couldn't knock. No one would be able to answer because the sunlight would come pouring through the door. Instead, he stood close to the door, listening intently for the sound of breathing or moving. But, as he was about to make his way to the top balcony to listen outside Astrid's window, he smelled the faint smell of smoke from inside.

He panicked and opened the door wide, ready to put out any flames he saw or kill whoever was making them. But to his surprise, as he opened the door, he saw Astrid standing in the diluted rays of the sun, burning pancakes on the stove.

Chapter 26

Carter shut the door fast and ran quickly over to Astrid. "You have to get out of the sun!" he shouted, holding tightly to her arm.

But Astrid simply wiggled him off and opened the window blinds brighter.

"It's fine," she said, holding her arm out to the entering rays. Carter held her arm in amazement. There were no burns, or red marks, or anything. The sun was doing no damage to her skin.

"Did Duncan make you a potion?" Carter asked, still perplexed by her skin safely resting in the sunlight.

"No," she answered. "The light just doesn't bother me. When Marcello and I returned home last night, it was close to dawn. Marcello became sleepy as he always does, and we both went up to our rooms to escape the returning light. But I couldn't sleep. I was too hungry.

"So, I wanted to take a quick peek outside to see if the sun was up yet. If not, I was going to run into the basement and grab a blood bag. But, as I opened the window and the rays hit my face, I felt no pain.

"For a while, I experimented, trying to see what was going on. But no matter what I did, or how much sun I was in, I never burned." She talked as she tossed a pancake off the pan and into the trash. But although she had burnt one, there was a huge plate full of butter-covered pancakes ready to be eaten. And that confused Carter as much as her unburned skin did.

"Why are you making pancakes?" he asked, switching the subject from her day-walking abilities to her newfound interest in making food as a vampire.

She looked down at the pile of food while resting the hot pan in the sink to cool. But she shook her head to signal her lack of an answer. "I don't know," she said, still staring at the full plate. "Once the fear of burning was completely gone, I went downstairs to get a blood bag. I drank the whole thing, amused by my sudden craving for blood. But I was still hungry, not for blood, though. I wanted human food. So, I ate a big bowl of cereal earlier, and now I'm hungry for pancakes."

She said all that with a strange amusement in her eyes. At first, he didn't understand why she was so calm and satisfied, even though so many strange things were happening since she was a vampire. He would have been terrified and very skeptical if all those things happened the first day he turned. But then Carter remembered: she had survived her twenty-fifth birthday for the first time in over two thousand years.

"I can't believe you remember me," she said, as if she had read his thoughts. She stood staring at him in amazement. Then, unexpectedly, tears filled her eyes. She covered her face in her hands, and instinctually, Carter wrapped her in his arms. "I'm just so happy," she said, fighting through her tears. She was surprised at how emotional she was. But then she remembered young vampires often had trouble dealing with the new, intense emotions of being a vampire.

He held her tightly in his arms, and she held on just as strongly, the tears uncontrollably falling from her eyes. She had never been so happy in her life. She felt Carter's eyes looking down at her, and she looked up through her tears to meet him. All of a sudden, her tears of happiness stopped flowing. The look in his eyes gave her the urge to be touched, to feel his skin against hers, and to feel his fangs pierce through her neck.

Carter saw the quick change in her eyes, and he knew that look. But as he went to romantically carry his crying love off her feet and take her sweetly to her room, she clung tightly to his collar and pushed him hard against the counter behind him.

The shock of her strength put him off, but the electric look in her eyes quickly put him back in the mood. He quickly picked her up and laid her roughly on the floor, holding her arms down tightly. But to his surprise, Astrid flipped him quickly over on his back, placing him in the same helpless position on the floor.

He pushed against her hands with all his strength, and without making an effort, Astrid held him down, not even noticing his struggle to get free. His expression changed again, and Astrid loosened up for only a second to make sure he was okay. He was blown away by her strength. Newborns were the weakest of all vampires, but she could've probably squashed him if she wanted to.

"You're so strong," he said while she looked curiously at his expression.

"Does that worry you?" she asked, lightly kissing his neck.

"It's just," he started, "newborns are never this strong."

"Oh?" she said, still kissing his bare neck. "Is there any chance you want to talk about this later?"

He thought about it for a second, then a wave of pleasure rushed through his body as he felt her soft lips caressing his neck.

"Yes," he answered. "We can definitely talk about that later."

***

After spending the day together, they recomposed themselves as the sun went down and sat on the second-floor balcony while they were waiting for Marcello to wake up. On top of all the other strange traits Astrid had, Carter also discovered that her blood was similar enough to human blood that he could still feed off of her. Quite frankly, Carter had simply discovered that Astrid was a vampire enigma, and he couldn't assume anything with her.

When Marcello woke up and made his way to the balcony with the couple, he was surprised to see Astrid drinking a glass of lemonade. She laughed a little at his confused looked and tried to explain that she wasn't a normal vampire.

For a moment, he stood in disbelief, and Astrid was worried he might be angry or frightened at her differences; his face was temporarily unreadable. But after a few awkward moments, he looked at Astrid sweetly and said, "I can't believe you're still here." She stood up quickly and gave him a big hug. They had waited so long for that day. They had both almost given up that it would ever happen.

"We should go see Duncan," Astrid said as she reached her hand out to Carter. "I've got to thank him with a big kiss or something," she said with a laugh. "Oh and also Sara. She is my creator after all."

They all made their way to Carter's house. But when they arrived, only Grayson and Sara were awake, and they both looked tense. Carter was the first to speak. "Is everything okay?" he asked, cautiously making his way to the living room area where Sara and Grayson were both standing defensively.

"Everything's fine," Grayson said with a growl, and he made his way upstairs.

Sara stood still for a moment with her head down.

"Where's Duncan?" Astrid asked, feeling very compassionate for Sara.

Sara had become Astrid's creator, and Astrid felt a new connection to her friend. She walked over to Sara, ready to find a private place where they could talk. But Sara wasn't in the mood to connect with her new protégée.

"He was really tired this morning," she answered, moving away from Astrid. "He hasn't left his room yet." And in a flash, she was out of the door.

"That was weird," Marcello said, breaking the awkward and confused silence that had filled the room.

Astrid just shook her head. She was extra hurt that Sara had shown no sign of being interested in Astrid, but she decided to not let it bother her.

"I'm going to go wake up Duncan," Astrid said, making her way up the stairs. Although the door was technically locked, her impulsive strength got the best of her, and she broke the door knob off, rendering the door lockless. She paused and her face showed signs of regret. But she giggled as she lightly pushed open the door, calling Duncan's name, a strange creature caught her eye.

She stood still for a moment, caught off guard by the pale, black-eyed being looking at her fearfully. But the voice and fear that came from its mouth allowed Astrid to realize who it was. "What are you doing?" Duncan screamed, covering his face and rushing over to shut the door. "Get out!"

But Astrid stuck out her hand to hold open the door. It had been quite an interesting first day as a vampire, and it was only getting weirder. "What happened to you, Duncan?" she said in a reassuring tone. She didn't want him to think she was scared of him. But he was too ashamed to be seen, and he slammed the door closed with a spell and sent Astrid flying to the floor. Then he bound the door shut so no one could get in.

Carter and Marcello reacted to the loud sounds upstairs and came up quickly to find Astrid sitting on the floor. She helped herself up and looked over at her friends. "Everyone in this house has gone insane," she said. "We should have stayed home."

Marcello and Carter weren't sure what had happened between Duncan and Astrid, but instead of explaining, Astrid stood close to the door and began talking. "Duncan, I just want to help," she said, hoping he was listening.

He could have bound the door to block the sound, and she hoped she wasn't wasting her breath. Still, Duncan didn't answer.

His silence frustrated Astrid, but she tried to remain sympathetic. "I just wanted to thank you," she said, deciding to ignore the strange. "I've been alive for over two thousand years, and I can honestly say today is the happiest day of my life. To be free of that curse… it's an indescribable feeling of happiness and relief."

Although he had also killed Mura and Jazel, the relief she felt was purely the free feeling she had of the curse leaving her body.

The silence was enough for her to know that he needed space. Or that maybe he didn't hear her. Either way, she left him upstairs, alone in his room, and decided to go look for Sara. "Does Sara have a place she goes to relax or regain her thoughts?" Astrid asked Carter.

"Well," he started, having to think, "sometimes, she goes downtown to sit at the bar. She's the only one of us who can still tolerate human things, and she'll sip drinks."

Astrid gave Carter a small kiss on the cheek and gave Marcello a big smile. Then she rushed out the door to find Sara, hoping to find out why her creator was so distressed.

When she arrived downtown, she walked over to The Casket and saw Carter had guessed correctly. Sara was sitting at the main bar, sipping on a whiskey sour, looking rather displeased. Astrid came over quietly and took the seat next to Sara without saying anything. Sara noticed her presence but didn't react to the new company.

Astrid didn't order anything. She just sat there quietly, hoping Sara would acknowledge her presence soon. And after a while, she finally did.

"What are you doing here?" Sara asked, finishing off the last sip of her drink.

"I wanted to see if you were okay," Astrid said, looking over at her friend. "I can feel when you're upset."

"Yeah, and I can feel your overwhelming happiness," Sara said jealously. But Astrid's kind eyes caused Sara to calm down a bit. "I just hate it; you know; being a vampire. You seem so happy about it. And I hate it. I don't see why Duncan can break your curse, but he can't find a way to turn me human again." She looked over sadly at Astrid. "I'm happy for you. I really am. I couldn't wait to break your curse. But it just reminds me of how much I hate being a vampire because now I can feel how happy you are with it, and it makes me sick."

Astrid wasn't sure what to say to Sara. She didn't know how to reassure someone who hated what they had become. She began to think of what Duncan looked like earlier when she saw him. She hoped he had found peace with the change that had happened. "Why were you and Grayson fighting?" Astrid asked. She thought maybe getting Sara to talk would make her feel better.

"Because like you, he's happy to be a vampire. I told him now that your curse was broken, maybe we could try to find a way to change vampires back into humans. He took that as an insult. But it has nothing to do with him. It's me. I don't want to be like this anymore. Honestly, I don't even know if I want to be with Grayson. If I could become a human again, I would run to another country, away from all the vampires and supernatural creatures I know, and just live a new, regular, human life."

Astrid hadn't known Sara was so displeased with her life as a vampire. She could understand it, though. Although some humans chose to become vampires, it was often not a choice. And Sara was one who was not given the right to choose.

So Astrid said she was sorry for Sara's pain and gave her a small hug before leaving the bar. She headed back to Sara's house to find Duncan and to see if he was willing to try and break one more person's curse. But first, she had to convince him to come out of his room.

Chapter 27

Astrid sat outside Duncan's door all night long. Carter and Marcello didn't completely understand why she was trying so hard to get him to come outside, but she wasn't interested yet in explaining it to them. So the men stayed up all night chatting while Astrid pestered Duncan through his door.

To her surprise, he never used a spell to shut her up and make her go away. And she knew he was listening because she would hear him laugh sometimes at her jokes. Since he wouldn't talk back, Astrid basically told stories all night. Mostly, they were funny. But a few hours before sunrise, she began to tell sad stories, ones she hoped he could relate with. Stories of sacrifice, hope, and change.

And then she told a story no one had ever heard before. "Everyone here thought Jazel looked terrifying," Astrid began. "And it was somewhat true. She had a darkness about her. But when I first saw her, she didn't frighten me at all. She actually reminded me of a friend I had growing up before I was cursed.

"I used to play around outside at night, even though I wasn't really supposed to. But I wasn't scared of the dark. The mystery drew me in, and once everyone had gone to sleep, I would sneak outside and explore the hidden world.

"Because this fear of the dark didn't exist, I was able to witness things most people never do. I knew about werewolves,

Naturals, vampires, and ghosts before I knew how to write or read or tell time. They would explore with me in the darkness, and the ones who were kind would protect me if anything evil were to appear in the dark. One evening, I had planned to meet a small ghost friend of mine."

Duncan shivered at the idea of their being real ghosts in the world. But Astrid made them seem kind and friendly.

"But I ran into another glowing figure who seemed more scared of me than I was of her. She hid behind a tree, and instead of running away, I sat down on the ground using the moonlight to draw pictures of animals in the loose dirt.

"Eventually, she came out from behind the tree, curious about what I was doing. She hesitated and asked why I wasn't scared of her. And I told her she hadn't given me any reason to be afraid I picked up another stick from the ground and motioned for her to take it so she could draw with me.

"It turned out this young girl was the first Natural I ever met. Her eyes were pitch black, and her skin was so white it glowed. After a few years together, I met another Natural, an older man, in the darkness. But when my friend appeared, the Natural I had just met killed her quickly, without even blinking. I screamed and ran to my friend, who was dead on the ground. But I had no strength or powers then, so all I could do was cry and ask why this Natural had just killed my friend.

"He told me she was a Natural of the Shadows, meaning her magic was dark, and that made her evil. But do you know what I actually learned that day?"

Duncan had moved close to the bound door, listening intently to her story. He shook his head no, answering her question, even though he knew she couldn't see.

"I learned that supernatural beings are just like people, every single one. They judge, and they assume, and they choose whether to be good or evil. My friend who had died used dark magic, but she was the kindest person I ever met. She had chosen to use that kind of magic, but it didn't make her evil. The man who killed her was the cruel one You don't scare me, Duncan. And just because you used a Shadow spell, it doesn't mean you're evil. Jazel chose to use her magic for true darkness, but that doesn't mean you're anything like her."

Grayson slowly opened his door and looked over to where Astrid was sitting. At the same time, Carter and Marcello both peeked their heads around the corner of the staircase. Apparently, everyone had chosen to listen to that story. Duncan's door suddenly cracked open a little, signaling the binding spell was no longer in effect. Astrid took that as a sign to go in. However, when she entered, Duncan was not inside.

It worried her that Duncan was not in his room, but she hoped he was out making peace with his new transformation. She passed Marcello and Carter as she went down the stairs, and they followed her to the living room, with Grayson in their tracks. He had calmed down from his fight with Sara, though he wasn't interested yet in discussing what had happened.

Both Grayson and Carter expressed an interest in feeding, so Marcello rushed back to the house to grab a few blood bags for everyone to feed on. It would be light soon, but he had enough time to share a meal with his friends. Although he had a potion to walk in the day, he liked the consistency of sleeping and rising with the sunset, so he didn't want to use it all the time.

Soon after he left, Sara showed back up at the house, but she wasn't alone. With her was another vampire whose name was Jericho. Astrid had never met him before. Though, from their short conversation before Marcello returned, he seemed like a nice, gentle guy. He didn't have any kind of daylight potion, so Sarah had offered him the house for the night while he was in town.

Apparently, he was an old friend of Grayson's and had visited a few times since they had lived in Blessings. All seemed to be going very well until Marcello returned.

He entered the door, carrying four small blood bags. He had a smile on his face when he saw Astrid, and she greeted him with a similar expression of happiness.

Marcello didn't notice Jericho when he first entered the room, though Jericho saw him almost instantly. Sara noticed the change in his expression; his face was filled with rage. But before she could say anything, and before Marcello could react, Jericho lunged toward Marcello with a strong stake in his hand.

And before Marcello could defend himself, it was too late. The end of a wooden stake stuck out of his chest, while the rest lay still in his heart. The room grew quiet, except for Astrid's shout of, "No!" as she rushed over toward Marcello.

Jericho stepped back, his face filled with relief. Astrid held tightly to Marcello as he fell to the ground. They were both in shock. She didn't know what to do, so she held him close to her. She couldn't take her eyes off his. He only had a few seconds before he turned to ash. Her eyes filled with water, though she made no sounds of crying. The tears simply rolled down her face, dripping softly on her clothes.

Marcello's eyes did the same, water streaming down from the sides. He looked into her eyes, and smiled his perfect sweet smile, and whispered Astrid's name as his eyes closed. Then only white ash was left, clinging to Astrid's body.

She clenched her hands tightly around the powdery substance. She doubled over where she sat, unable to breathe or move. All she felt was a sharp pain in her chest pulsing through her whole body. It felt like a stake was in her heart too.

Her mood changed quickly. Her face shot up, her eyes a strange purple color, something no one had ever seen before.

Her fangs were out, and her eyes were locked on Jericho, who looked afraid.

She slammed him hard up against the wall. Her strength was much greater than his, and he couldn't resist the attack. She gave a low growl, holding the stake he had killed Marcello with. But before she could attack, Grayson called for mercy. She paused for a moment, with far more rage in her eyes than Jericho had ever had in his.

"At least let him explain," Grayson pleaded for his friend's life. "He's my creator."

She didn't let him go. But she loosened her grip just enough so he could breathe, signaling him to explain himself.

He stuttered out of fear for his life as he spoke. "Four hundred and fifty-six years ago," he started, "that man killed my life partner. She was the only woman who ever meant anything to me. She was my creator and my companion."

Astrid waited for a moment to see if he wanted to explain his story any more. But then she realized she didn't care.

"Well," Astrid began, "you just killed the only person who was ever able to keep me rational. Looks like bad luck for you." And then she killed him.

She ripped out the stake, throwing it fast to the ground. She didn't even look back at her friends in the room. She didn't care anymore. She vanished out of the door before another word could be said.

***

Duncan had woken up in the middle of the night only to notice he no longer looked like himself. He had changed into that terrifying creature he had seen a few times before. He bound himself in his room, refusing to leave or speak to anyone. But Astrid had come over, sitting outside his door and speaking to him all night. Her words *truly* spoke to him when she told her last story about the Natural she had befriended as a child.

When Duncan realized Astrid's story was over, he decided she was right. He didn't feel evil or dark. He just felt powerful. And he wanted to use that power to do good things.

He had heard Sara and Grayson fighting earlier. And he had heard Sara complain many times before that she didn't want to be a vampire. She had said it before she was even turned. So Duncan decided to take action.

He could no longer hide that he had used a Shadow spell. So he unbound his room and transported himself into the basement of the bookstore his mother guarded. He was able to get past the spell that prevented people from entering the basement.

When he arrived, he could feel the words of every Shadow calling to him. He wanted to read every book and hold tight to everyone. But instead, he focused all of his energy on what he wanted to accomplish with a spell and waited 'till a Shadow book began to call his name.

It didn't take long for a Shadow to try and reveal itself to him. He walked over to the back shelf of the room and found the book now glowing with energy.

As he picked up the book, it instantly opened, showing him the spell he needed to allow Sara to return to her human form. But as the words entered his mind, he closed the book in horror. Unlike most spells and Shadows, that one didn't need the energy of the moon or of the sun. It required a very specific sacrifice.

He put the book back on the shelf and walked away. Although the words of the Shadow stuck deep in his mind, he knew he could never use it.

With his back turned to the stairs, he heard his mother's voice calling from the steps. "Who are you?" she said in a strong voice.

But Duncan simply vanished, leaving her alone and confused. He wasn't yet ready to show himself to her. He needed more time to adapt to the new skin he wore.

He returned to his home where two piles of white ash lay still on the floor, and Grayson sat on the couch bent over with his head in his hands. Sara sat by him, trying to comfort him. Carter, Astrid, and Marcello were nowhere to be seen. Fear shot through his mind as he wondered if those dead vampire ashes were theirs.

"What happened?" Duncan asked, walking over to his friends. Grayson kept his head down. Sara jumped at the sight of Duncan's new change, not completely realizing it was him. But that reaction caused Grayson to stir away from his grief, and he saw how Duncan looked. He remembered the story Astrid had said outside his door, and he knew it was Duncan.

"I see you were tired of being Black," Grayson said in an attempt to make Duncan feel better and hint to Sara that Duncan had changed.

"What happened to you?" Sara asked, still cautious of the strange person looking at her.

But Grayson returned to his position of grief, and his relaxing allowed Sara to feel safe.

"It's a long story," Duncan started, not in the mood to explain the whole situation. "What I want to know is who died in here?" He pointed to the two piles of ash

Sara told the story while Grayson continued to mourn.

Grayson was torn. He was angry at Astrid for killing his creator, but he couldn't help but sympathize with her reaction. Either way, he was sad about the loss of his friend.

Duncan, however, was shocked that Marcello had been killed. He tried to imagine the pain Astrid must have felt to watch her lifelong friend die right before her eyes. He wished he had been here to help. Maybe he could have saved him with some kind of spell.

He still wondered, though, where Carter had gone.

"He went to look for Astrid," Grayson said in a muffled voice, finally lifting his head from its position of grief. "I can't believe that just happened."

"Where have you been?" Sara asked.

He hesitated to answer. He wasn't sure what to tell her. But he trusted his friend, so he decided on the truth. "Honestly," he began, "I went to find a spell to change you into a human."

Sara's eyes lit up, although Grayson didn't look too happy.

"And?" she asked, eager to hear if he found anything.

"Well, I found a spell that would work," he said, "but we can't use it."

"Why not?" she asked, irritated she had been given false hope.

"Because we would have to kill Astrid."

Chapter 28

Carter found Astrid shortly after she disappeared from his house. She hadn't gone far. She was sitting quietly alone outside the pond behind her house. Her knees were pulled up tightly to her chest while her chin rested on them. The sounds of nature filled the air. It was a peaceful place to sit. Marcello had chosen a great place for them to live.

Carter came over to her side. She could smell and hear him coming, but she didn't care. Deep down, she was eager for the company but just too scared to ask for it. She felt lost and insecure without Marcello.

Carter sat down beside her, taking in the view around him. "Everything here is beautiful," he said. He glanced over at her while she looked out over the water. "Of course, nothing quite takes my breath away like you do."

His comment earned him an endearing glance but nothing more. After a few moments of silence, she finally stretched out her legs, resting her hands behind her back. She shook her head in disbelief. "I just can't believe he's gone," she said, still looking over the water. "Everything was perfect, and now…" she paused, her throat catching. She couldn't hold in her tears anymore. It felt like her chest was collapsing. She couldn't get in any breath.

Carter reached over quickly and held her close. The comfort of his body allowed the breath to finally flow in. They sat there for a while, and she cried every tear she needed to for Marcello. It was all she could do to honor his death. They both had the same thought that only a day earlier she was crying in Carter's arms. But before, it was out of happiness. This was out of grief.

By the time the sun went down, Carter suggested they return to his house. She wondered if Grayson would even want to see her after what she had done, but he assured her it would be okay. Grayson had acted on his emotions many times in his vampire life. He would understand her reaction, even if the loss of his creator hurt him.

Astrid agreed to come with Carter, but she asked for a few moments alone.

"I'll meet you in a bit," she said. "I just need a few minutes by myself."

Carter gave her a reassuring smile and kissed her on the forehead before taking off to his house. She let out a few more tears for her friend, speaking only to herself that she would miss him greatly.

After she made her peace, she stood up and walked over slowly to Carter's house. She was a vampire. She had all the time in the world. She didn't need to rush.

***

"What?" Sara asked in disbelief.

"In order for the spell to work properly," he began, "a vampire who wishes to become a human again must kill one of their protégé. In this case, that would be Astrid." Duncan didn't even consider for a second that he would kill Astrid. He cared too much about her, and she had done so much for them, especially after losing Marcello.

Sara looked thoughtfully at Duncan. It was a strangely scary look for him to see. He wondered if she was considering that killing Astrid may be an option. But he knew Sara would never think like that. Still, he wondered what strange thoughts were crossing her mind.

Once the nighttime settled in, Carter returned to the house.

"Is Astrid okay?" Grayson asked, looking concerned.

Everyone was shocked that he was the first one to ask that question, and he noticed the look of confusion in everyone's eyes.

"Yes," he started, "I'm angry with her. But I've thought about it all day, and the reality is, Marcello was everything to her. Jericho was my creator, which meant a lot to me, but not as much as Marcello meant to her. So yes, I want to know if she's okay."

Carter didn't hesitate after that. "She'll be fine," he said. "She's coming over soon. She needed some time by herself first."

"We should celebrate," Sara said randomly.

Everyone looked at her, surprised.

"It hasn't been the best day," she admitted, "but Mura and Jazel are dead, the Willow family can never bother us again, and Astrid's curse has been broken. I think those are things worth celebrating."

Although no one necessarily agreed, Sara fished out the blood bags Marcello had brought over and no one had eaten. She poured everyone a glass, even one for Astrid, whenever she showed up, although she didn't give one to Duncan. Instead, she retrieved a cold beer from the fridge and handed it to him.

Everyone hesitated for a moment, unsure if it was really the time to celebrate. But when Astrid walked in a few seconds later, she smiled at the joy on Sara's face, and at all her friends gathered in the room. They decided then that maybe it was a time to rejoice at their accomplishments and at the freedom they had.

Sara handed Astrid a glass of blood, and she took it with a smile. A great sense of hope filled her body, especially after Grayson gave her a pat on the back. Their eyes locked for a moment, and they each said they were sorry without saying any words.

Although Marcello was gone, she was left with a great sense of family and community. The love Marcello had given her filled the room, filling her up as well. And the new friends she had made were the kind of friends she could keep for life. She had felt so alone when Marcello died, but she felt like she would never be alone again.

But as she turned her back to Sara, giving Carter a big smile, the same stake that killed Marcello and Jericho stuck through her heart. The only words she could think to say as she saw Carter's shocked face reaching for her body were, "I love you."

Everyone backed away from Sara, watching as Carter held Astrid's dying body. Her eyes closed and they all expected her to turn to ash, but she didn't. Instead, her body went cold. He felt her heart stop and her breathing cease. She was dead, but her body still didn't turn to ash.

Carter looked viciously at Sara. "What's wrong with you?" he screamed, tears filling his eyes.

Sara stood, watching the faint stain of blood on her hand. She ignored Carter and looked over quickly at Duncan.

"There," she said, pointing to Astrid's lifeless body. "My protégée is dead. Now you can use the spell to make me human again."

Carter didn't know what she was talking about, but Duncan couldn't shake his face of shock.

"I… I can't," he said, looking over sadly at Astrid. He regretted ever telling Sara about the spell. She would have never killed Astrid if he hadn't.

"Why not?" she shouted. "I did what you said I needed to do, so now you can turn me back."

Carter looked at Duncan furiously, but he refused to be blamed for Astrid's death.

"I told you I wouldn't use the spell because Astrid would have to die," he said, clarifying he had never told Sara to kill Astrid.

"Well it's too late now," Sara said. "Unless you want her to have died for no reason, you should go ahead and use the spell."

But Duncan knew it was wrong. "No matter what I do," Duncan started, "Astrid's death will be in vain."

She stood in disbelief that Duncan would refuse to change her back into a human. Her mind had been warped greatly by her vampire transformation, more than anyone had realized. "So you won't change me back?" she asked, sadness in her voice.

"No," Duncan said firmly.

Carter couldn't take any more. "Get out!" he shouted to Sara. "Get out now!"

But she didn't leave. She simply made her way upstairs and locked herself in her room. She knew her friends would forgive her. It would just take time. They had all done terrible things in their lives at one time or another. They couldn't even judge that one action she had taken to return herself to humanity. And deep down, after they witnessed the event, they all knew they would someday forgive her.

But that day was far off. Carter looked down desperately at Astrid. He kept waiting for her to wake up, but she never did.

He held her for two days, not eating or sleeping while he waited. She had to wake up. Her body had not turned to ash. She couldn't be dead. But after two days, Grayson convinced him it was time to put her to rest.

They went to her house and dug a large grave near the banks of her pond, placing her gently inside. Duncan joined them after they had finished, though Sara stayed at home, keeping her distance.

Carter couldn't stand to see her sitting in that cold hole in the ground. He still didn't believe she was dead. But he couldn't keep hoping forever that she would wake up. Grayson handed him the shovel, and Carter laid the first cover of dirt over her beautiful body.

When they finished, Carter stayed there for a while. And Grayson sat with him. Carter told stories about Astrid's life that she had shared with him and told Grayson how much he had grown to care for her. "I loved her, Grayson," he said, looking like a sad, lost child. Grayson laid his hand on his friend's back, and they spent the rest of the time in silence.

***

A month passed, and the lives of Grayson, Carter, Duncan, and Sara had almost returned to normal. In one way or another, Sara managed to gain everyone's forgiveness, although their trust in her would be much harder to regain. And Carter was not as willing to forgive. He accepted she was so desperate to become human again that she would have done anything, like when someone commits suicide because they saw no other way out. But with Astrid dead, Sara could no longer return to being human. She had already killed her first protégée. She had to accept for good that she'd be a vampire forever.

All but Sara sat in the living room, waiting to feed. She had gone hunting and was soon to return with their meal of blood for the day. Duncan had already eaten his dinner. He didn't like eating while they were feeding on blood.

When she returned, they drained the small deer of blood. But before they had a chance to feed, something they never could have guessed happened.

Chapter 29

Astrid's eyes opened suddenly, instantly filling with a wet, coarse substance. She closed them again, confused. She lay there silently, feeling the cool, damp texture surrounding her bare hands, a heavy pressure crushing her body. The smell then became obvious: dirt. She was underground, buried maybe. She couldn't remember what had happened or why she was there. She wasn't scared but knew she needed to get out.

The pressure on her body was the same all around; she couldn't tell which way she was facing. It reminded her of stories she had heard where people drowned because they swam the wrong way underwater. It was too dark to see, and everything felt the same around her. But she decided to take a gamble, hoping whoever put her here had the decency to bury her facing up.

To test how far down she was buried, she tried to move her arms, but with only a little strength. The dirt was heavy, and her arms barely moved. She was hopefully only a few feet underground; she wasn't really interested in digging through the dirt for hours. So using her full strength, she began to thrash and claw at the cocoon of dirt ensnaring her body.

The experience of digging herself out of the ground was not a pleasant one. She was used to seeing in the dark, but the dirt was in her way, stinging as it scratched at her eyes. It made her feel helpless and blind.

And although she had no reason to fear death, it was daunting to be unsure if she was digging herself to the surface or deeper underground.

After only a few seconds of digging, she noticed the ground above her feeling lighter, when suddenly, one hand reached desperately above the ground, and the cool breeze brushed over her hand, sending waves of relief over her body. She freed her other hand then hoisted herself quickly above the ground. She lay there for a moment, feeling the freedom and space all around her, allowing the sight of the stars to give her comfort.

It was then, serenely lying on the ground, that she became aware; it was then that she remembered.

Cautiously, she placed her hands on her chest directly above her heart, finally noticing the faint blood smell mixed in with the dirt. She sat up, feeling the small hole in her clothes where the stake had pierced her heart; her body jerked, and she let out a groan as if she had been stabbed all over again.

She didn't know how long she had been buried or what day it was, but the pain and anger she felt was the one thing she was certain about. Her friend, one she had opened her heart to, one who had helped break her curse, one she thought had loved her, betrayed her, literally stabbing a stake into her heart. And for what? She didn't know. But she remembered it all.

Her next step became clear. Her eyes narrowed and focused. All the restraints were gone. She took her time, though, standing up slowly. She glanced at her body smeared with black dirt, and the hole where she had been stabbed healed. She didn't know why she was alive or how she had survived being staked. But right then, she didn't care. A pulsing rage shot through her body.

She took her time walking to where Sara lived. The path she chose would be the most direct route, going straight through downtown. It was nighttime, so not very many people would be out. The ones who were out would be distracted by their beers in the bar. It didn't matter anyway. After that night, she would never return to that town again.

She realized there was one last thing she needed to do before she went to see Sara. So she began to make her way over to her house. As she reached the front steps, she gave the house a good look over. It was a nice place to live; small, quiet, and beautiful. Marcello had chosen well. She first walked around back, grabbed the small gas can that rested near the lawn mower, and then headed inside her house. She punctured a nickel-sized hole in the can and began to pace around her halls.

The house was fairly clean, except for the few random weapons lying around. She saw her favorite gun sitting on the dining room table. She rarely used it, but it was a nice weapon to have.

Her hand grazed over it, feeling the curves and texture, sending shockwaves through her body. It was small, just a little bigger than her hand. But its magically crafted wooden bullets always did the trick. And she never missed.

In a blink, she was standing in the open front door, staring into what was once her home; in one hand, her gun, and in the other, a violent purple-colored zippo lighter ready to burn.

She stood there for a second. Not hesitating, just taking in the moment. She felt good; powerful and in control. She flipped open the lighter across her mud-stained jeans and flicked on the flame. In one swift move, she tossed the lighter into the gasoline-drenched house, turned, and walked away, never looking back.

She could feel the heat as the wooden house was taken by the flames, never once stopping to wonder what Marcello would have thought of all this.

Her body moved toward, and through, the woods. She was no longer in control of herself. Her feeling, her passion, the pulses that had begun when she remembered the truth, were in control. The air was cooling ever so slightly as she stepped cautiously over the twigs and roots, weaving her way almost fluid-like through the trees.

As she divulged herself from the woods, she made her way down the narrow gravel driveway to Sara's house; the lights were all on, like they were all inside expecting her. She could hear their whispers through the walls. They spoke of regrets, sadness, and disappointment; it felt good to hear Sara's last words.

She wisped up the stone stairs, moving like mist. She twisted the locked silver doorknob, barely noticing the loud crack it made as she broke the lock.

As she pushed open the door, she moved with its movement, never once pausing.

The gasps from the living room reached her ears; the swiftness of two protective male vampires greeted her at the door. She walked right past them as they stood dumbfounded by her presence and appearance.

She made her way into the dimly lit living room, pausing only to see her eyes one last time; she would never forget that look. It was the look of confusion, fear, and then suddenly, realization. But before Sara could let out a plea for help or forgiveness, Astrid lifted her gun, aimed it at Sara's rapidly beating heart, and fired.

The Hunter's Curse